The gun barrel came up hard against the base of his skull

Carl Lyons was a tough man. He'd exchanged blows with bigger, meaner brawlers and still managed to come out on top. But tonight the Able Team warrior's knees gave out as bolts of pain lanced through both temples.

He slammed, facefirst, onto the rooftop. Lyons's head was jerked back and his eyeballs rolled up into his brain, where thoughts scattered in terror and his mind tumbled head over heels into the black abyss.

Mack Bolan's

ABLE TEAM

ABLE TEAM.
Counterblow

Dick Stivers

A GOLD EAGLE BOOK FROM
WORLDWIDE.

TORONTO • NEW YORK • LONDON • PARIS
AMSTERDAM • STOCKHOLM • HAMBURG
ATHENS • MILAN • TOKYO • SYDNEY

Dedicated to
the suffering children
of Indochina

First edition February 1990

ISBN 0-373-61246-X

Special thanks and acknowledgment to
Nicholas Cain for his contribution to this work.

Printed in U.S.A.

1

She was tall and blond, with voluptuous curves and long, sleek legs that went on forever. But when she walked through the cavernous lounge, balancing a rocket launcher across her wrists, none of the dozen men present seemed to notice her. Their eyes were on the two wrestlers seated under the glittering Chinese dragon lantern, and the scorpions that danced in tight circles beneath their clasped fists on the round white marble table.

"Fifty bucks on Donovan!"

"Double that! Nunn's got him by the balls—now his heart and mind *will* follow! No contest, man!"

"*Hundred* and fifty on the big merc."

"Double that! No way Nunn's gonna let me down. Are ya, Nunn?"

The dozen or so members of the Adventurers Club—currently gathered in one of the many lounges of its penthouse quarters located in one of New York's seedier industrial neighborhoods—circled the marble table. They slapped their sheathed bayonets and calf daggers in anticipation as they produced bundles of greenbacks, continuing the rapid-fire exchange of wagers. In the smoke-choked background the tall blonde reached her destination and loudly dropped the rocket launcher onto the long, winding counter of the bar.

"Told you so," the big man said, producing a smile as he polished empty beer mugs with a dishrag.

"Eat it," the woman responded with an obscene gesture before pulling out a well-concealed pocketbook. Shifting her shapely hips into a provocative, defensive stance, she focused on the mirror running the length of the wall behind the bartender. She concentrated on the cluster of men gathered around the two arm wrestlers fifty feet away as she surrendered a hundred-dollar bill.

"Thank you, ma'am," the bartender said, laughing. He was a bronzed bodybuilder with short curly black hair, a jutting jaw and scars crisscrossing one cheek. The scars were souvenirs of his MP days, battling race riots in Seoul, Korea. Tattoos of a charging rogue elephant adorned both bulging biceps.

The woman's eyes flickered in his direction—she judged him to be in his mid-forties, Vietnam material, or perhaps a Rhodesian bush vet—then returned to the men cheering on the two arm wrestlers. She watched the continual exchange of money as their excitement grew. The loser risked being stung by one of the black rhino scorpions, and blue veins bulged along the foreheads of both contestants when their arms dipped closer to the cool marble.

"Why do they do it, Glenn?"

The bartender's smile faded only slightly as he removed the rocket launcher from the counter and placed it inside one of the beer coolers. "Arm wrestle? For money, dear. Purely money."

"Not the challenge? The risk?"

"Oh, there's certainly danger associated with the scorpions, if that's what you mean . . ."

"Of course that's what I mean." The woman was in her mid-twenties, but her expression suggested she'd had considerable experience dealing with hardened men and tough situations. In reality Joan Charlotte Andrews had never flirted face-to-face with Lady Death—she'd never really earned the right to drink at the Adventurers Club, to party or celebrate or conduct business in its exotically decorated and expensively furnished lounge. Her father, Roy Chatsworth Andrews, was current president of the New York branch of the international organization—he had been for the past twenty years. *That* afforded Joan, his daughter, certain lifelong privileges, which no one had ever challenged.

She'd spent much of her teenage years at the Club, listening to men fresh in from Africa, India or the Orient exchange war stories or detailed accounts of their latest expedition or discovery. Since allowing female members of exceptional character and a proven thrill-seeker's track record to join in the late seventies, Joan's presence in the formerly all-male domain no longer turned heads as it once had.

Thus, she had to resort to new tricks, elaborate games, now and then. Waltzing through the lobby with the rocket launcher had been her own idea. Glenn the bartender was confident even *that* would fail to attract attention when Big Don Donovan and Peter K. Nunn were going at it on "center stage."

The black rhino scorpions were an unusually large species native to Southeast Asia and other tropical segments of the globe. One sting could be quite painful—several could result in paralysis, coma and, eventually, death. If the stings went untreated.

"They do it for the hell of it," Glenn said, glancing over at the men gathered at the table. "Because they're tired of the hurry-up-and-wait routine of Chad or Angola or Afghanistan merc recruitments and need a little simple entertainment—something stateside with an overseas flavor to it."

"But those scorpions..." Joan sighed and allowed her shoulders to droop in surrender as she sat down on one of the bar stools.

"The trick is to..." Glenn began, placing his elbow on the counter in front of her, fist raised in an arm wrestling position. "Well, when you fear you're about to lose...that your opponent is getting the best of you, gaining leverage—you slam them knuckles down, baby!" His fist struck the counter with a sudden, vicious impact. "And squash that bug before it can bite you!"

No sooner had he explained the strategy than Nunn delivered a sharp, cracking blow to the white marble tabletop in the center of the lounge.

"Oh, bummer, dude!" someone groaned with mock concern, his favorite "surfer boy" accent rising to the surface.

"What happened?" Joan asked, glancing back over her shoulder. "Did he...?"

Nunn rose from the table, shaking his head from side to side and clutching his discolored arm. After digging into a pocket, he withdrew a handful of dollars, slammed them down on the remains of the dead scorpion and stalked over toward the bar.

"It got 'im!" Glenn said. "Better bring out the firewater." He lifted a bottle of special whiskey from under the counter.

"The scorpion bit him?" Joan gasped softly, prepared to move away—Nunn seemed to be heading straight for her section of the bar.

"Ol' Nunn just wasn't quick enough this time." Glenn laughed again.

"Damned if I know how you clowns always sucker me into arm-wrestling Donovan, *anyway*!" Nunn said as he claimed a stool on Joan's right. He was a big man in his early thirties, with a deceptive, babyish face and close-cropped hair that had a premature gray hue to it.

"Are you going to be all right?" Joan asked, fighting the instinct to move away from the man and his rough-looking entourage. Instead, she took his arm in her dainty, uncal-lused hands. "It's really starting to swell. Maybe we should get you to an emergency room."

"Nonsense!" Donovan, who had just moved up to the bar, took hold of her arms from behind, gently removing her from the stool, which he then claimed. She didn't argue with the notorious mercenary—he was bigger than Nunn, with a sinister-looking Zapata mustache that hung on either side of his chin like black, tightly bound wires. Although he was able to grow a full head of hair if the notion struck him, Donovan kept his crown shaved as smooth as a baby's bottom—as smooth as the shrapnel scars here and there would allow.

"*Nonsense?*" Joan Andrews protested.

"Do I stutter, woman?" Donovan reached down and drew a sparkling commander dagger from its calf sheath. His free fist lashed out and took hold of Nunn's wrist.

Joan watched as he quickly slashed a neat *X* over the throbbing scorpion sting before the other man could protest. Blood and pus spurted forth, and Joan gasped again—this time louder.

"You're not going to—" Joan began.

"Correct," Donovan said, grinning. "*I'm* not gonna do nothing! *Charlie Cope!* Front and center!"

Charlie Cope was the newest initiate to the New York faction of the International Adventurers Club and, as such, was subject to demeaning chores, rituals and ceremonies during his first month as a member. He was a short, bent, worried-looking man in his early fifties, with a receding hairline, thick, black-framed glasses and a pronounced limp. His claim to fame was the recent discovery of a deep maze of caves—in Jamaica, which included the hideout of a gang of black drug runners. He shot six of them when they jumped his own group, looking for an easy supply of provisions. "What do you expect me to do?" Charlie Cope asked, gaping at the ugly wound.

"Pretend it's a rattlesnake bite," Donovan decided.

"You mean . . . suck out the poison?"

"Give the man a mail-order Ph.D.," Glenn snickered from behind the false protection of the bar. He handed the bespectacled explorer a small rubber contraption often found in snakebite kits. "Use this."

"Always keep that around the bar?" Joan questioned, smiling up at him.

"In this place you have to," Glenn said, nodding.

For the first time Joan Andrews noticed two strangers amid the usually fraternal gathering of trouble chasers. She watched the bemused expressions of the well-built men.

"Drinks on Big Don!" the soldier of fortune yelled, raising a fistful of money to ease the tension crowding the bar.

"Booze, gentlemen?" Joan asked when she realized the two newcomers were staring back at her. They had that confident, inseparable look. "I don't believe we've had the pleasure...."

"Hermann Schwarz," the man with the neatly trimmed mustache and sky-blue eyes said as he extended a hand.

"His enemies call him Ugly," a tall, lean Hispanic with wavy, combed-back hair said. The hair had once been brown, but was now nearly white, giving him a wild, intimidating appearance Andrews found oddly exciting.

Schwarz's smile grew. "But you can call me Gadgets."

"And you?" Joan's eyes shifted to the other man.

"Rosario Blancanales," the light-skinned Hispanic answered, taking Andrews's hand and gently kissing her knuckles.

"*His* friends and enemies alike call him Politician," Schwarz said, laughing softly as the caps were twisted off beer bottles all around them.

With a discriminating eye Joan Andrews thought she spotted the telltale outline of concealed weapons beneath their black jean jackets, but didn't mention it. Instead, she said, "Gadgets? Dare I ask where you got such a—"

Blancanales winked. "He likes to tinker." Politician fought the involuntary urge to let his eyes drop for an inspection of her well-endowed curves.

"And this hombre enjoys talking his way out of bad situations," Schwarz returned, wrapping an arm around his buddy.

"Joan Andrews," she said, finally getting the chance to introduce herself. "You two look like cops to me." She grinned back, no disapproval in her look or tone. "Otherwise you'd never have gotten past our security. This is a private club, you know."

"Oh, we know, we know," Blancanales said, nodding.

"Big Don Donovan invited us over," Schwarz revealed. "Said he was gonna challenge Nunn to a little 'dance with the scorpions.'"

"Needless to say, we didn't think he meant—" Blancanales began.

"Yes," Andrews said, nodding in the wounded mercenary's direction. "I think 'dancing with death is sufficient,'" she continued, quoting one of her longtime heroines, Madame Nhu, South Vietnam's infamous dragon lady who was now exiled to Paris.

"They certainly know how to have a good time around here," Schwarz commented, his eyes scanning the maze of interconnecting penthouse suites. Several walls had obviously been knocked out to allow the top floor to serve as an open gathering place. He focused on a bloodstained AK-47 assault rifle hanging over one doorway in a glass-enclosed frame.

In large crimson letters below the war trophy an inscription read:

You have never lived until you have almost died. For those who fight for it, life has a flavor the protected will never know.

—Combat Zone Philosophy
Pleiku, Vietnam—1972

"I like that," he muttered under his breath. He returned his gaze to the bar and focused on an autographed photo hanging above the long mirror behind the bartender. Schwarz instantly recognized the grainy likeness of Ernest Hemingway, renowned adventurer and novelist.

"You're thinking of joining the Adventurers Club?" Joan asked Blancanales, who was examining the lavish tapestries and paintings hanging from every wall of the windowless lounge. "I suppose you're into...imports and exports," she said, laughing lightly.

"We're sort of..." Schwarz answered for his friend.

"Jacks of all the international trades," Blancanales added. He didn't bother to mention that they were members of Able Team, an elite counterterrorist squad only the President could call in when things got too tough for regular public servants to handle, or so hot that a deniability factor was needed. Able Team was always there, whenever the Pentagon required a group of highly trained sappers, familiar with the use and implementation of a variety of "sterile weapons"—men who could accept the fact that their missions were so ultrasecret that Washington would deny any knowledge of their existence should they be captured by the enemy or exposed by the media. To work in this field one had to make peace with oneself mentally, accept the inevitable fact that one's days on the street were numbered, long before donning the hardware of death. There was little talk of the future, only the present mission. It was a lifelong job with no easy retirement or pension perks. Often the only way out was in a body bag.

"Big Don suggested we apply to the Adventurers Club," Schwarz said, scanning the many tapestries now, examining scenes of safaris on the dark continent, sampan races in the steaming Orient, deep-sea diving through coral catacombs off Australia's Great Barrier Reef. All of the tapestries had been done in bright, almost psychedelic oils on purple felt. "We're not much when it comes to thrill-seeking or danger chasing, though," he added with a straight face.

"We kind of prefer a quiet night in the library," Blancanales said, nodding again. "Mystery section, of course."

"Of course," Gadgets returned with a tight grin.

"Well, we don't do a lot of reading around here," Joan Andrews said, her hand gesturing toward Donovan and Nunn. "They're the kind of men adventure novels are *written* about. They—"

"Yes, yes..." Blancanales interrupted her. "We can see that. The only reading material in sight is that rack of military magazines over there."

"That's how a lot of these guys keep in touch," Andrews revealed. "Through the Personals section of the Classifieds in the back."

"And you, Miss Andrews?" Schwarz asked. "What notorious deed did *you* commit to gain admittance to this rather chauvinistic den of—"

"My father runs the joint," she said simply.

"Oh..." Blancanales answered before leaning toward Donovan and Nunn, who were catching up on the latest bit of gossip to make Club rounds.

Batting her eyelashes at Gadgets, Joan Andrews excused herself from the bar. Schwarz zeroed in on her firm bottom and delicate, smoothly calculated footfalls as she headed for the ladies' room to freshen up. "Don't even think it," he heard Rosario's whisper. "Remember, she's the old man's little girl. I'd wager she's off-limits around here. Otherwise, these guys would all be—"

"Yeah, yeah," Gadgets said, waving his concern away. "Forget it. I can dream, can't I?"

Donovan's voice interrupted his thoughts. "And I'm telling you," the well-known soldier of fortune was saying, "them babies are worth about ten million greenbacks, easy!"

"What babies?" Gadgets asked. He had met Donovan at a recent firearms convention in Phoenix, and the two had become fast friends.

Donovan called the Big Apple home. His business card boasted that the Adventurers Club was his official haunt. "Look me up next time you're in New York City," he had declared. And they had—with a little added urging from the State Department.

"Huh?" Schwarz repeated now. "What babies?"

Big Don Donovan became silent, slowly turning to glance over a shoulder at the two Able Team commandos. "Emeralds," he answered, his eyes locking onto Schwarz suddenly, taking on a deadly seriousness that startled the Able Team veteran.

"Emeralds?" Gadgets's own eyes grew large and round. He felt Rosario's breathing quicken nearby.

"From the Kingdom of Siam, gents," Peter K. Nunn added.

"Siam?" Blancanales questioned.

"Now known as Thailand," Donovan said. "She produces more emeralds than steamed rice and king cobras combined."

"She?" Schwarz asked.

"The jungled hills north of Bangkok," Donovan revealed. "Caves deep in the heart of the rain forest outside Chiang Mai."

"Tell 'em about the rumors, Big Don," Nunn said, elbowing his fellow merc roughly.

Schwarz's eyes lit up. "Rumors?"

"What rumors?" Blancanales asked, echoing Gadgets.

"Rumors been circulating in professional adventurers' clubs throughout the United States about a cache of precious stones from Vietnam, gentlemen. Originally they were stolen from the Kingdom of Siam centuries ago, and hidden by their most recent owner—a general with the French Foreign Legion—some thirty-five years ago."

"French Foreign Legion?" Schwarz's enthusiasm *had* turned genuine. He'd always been fascinated by stories involving the Legionnaires.

"The French general," Donovan continued, "concealed the emeralds somewhere in an underground series of tunnels and caves in March 1954, shortly before he was killed during the battle for a hilltop known as Ann-Marie. The Viet Minh won that series of confrontations near Dien Bien Phu, as you know, leading to the disgrace of France and the eventual pullout of all French troops from Vietnam. Word trickling down the wait-a-minute vine in merc circles has it that the cache of jewels was uncovered sometime after the surrender of Saigon in 1975 and, more recently, has made its way to the United States...."

"Made its way?" Schwarz quipped, forcing a smile as he tried to ignore his partner's frown. "You mean, those goofy emeralds just *walked* on over to this here land of the free and home of the brave... just *tippy-toed* forth, or *what*?" Schwarz's grin became a sneer, his sudden irritation showing through. "Be specific, man—*specific*."

"Hey, mellow out," Blancanales cautioned, leaning closer to his longtime friend.

"Well, it just seems these guys are long on theatrics and short on substance," Gadgets complained.

"What a chump," Donovan said, starting to turn away.

"Forget him," Nunn agreed.

"Hey, we're listening," Blancanales argued.

"There's not much more to tell," Donovan said, motioning for the bartender to refill his glass. "Somewhere out there in never-never land there's ten million bucks worth of high-quality Asian emeralds...."

"And *we* aim to locate 'em," Nunn said, beaming. "One way or another."

"Any idea where you're going to start?" Schwarz asked, sounding somewhat skeptical.

"Sure, we've got an idea," Donovan answered, flexing his biceps.

"Better than that," Nunn said, his smile spreading from ear to ear. "We've got a map."

Donovan nonchalantly left his bar stool and sauntered over to the glass terrarium sitting atop an old, unplugged jukebox. Dozens of scorpions danced grotesque duets inside the desk-size container. Ignoring the deadly arachnids, Big Don reached in, brushed two of the creatures off a black lacquer jewelry box and lifted it out of the terrarium.

He extended the jewelry box toward Schwarz and Blancanales. "Kind of reminds you of *Treasure Island*, don't it?" His amused grin revealed two or three missing teeth.

"Depends on whether this so-called map of yours leads to anything or anyplace worthwhile," Blancanales answered, remaining unconvinced.

"Oh, it does...it does. It leads to a whole Pandora's box of juicy clues, mate." Donovan removed a chrome key from a chain around his neck and began to unlock the jewelry box when one of the side doors to the lounge burst open and two masked men, toting sawed-off shotguns, entered the Adventurers Club, shouting threats and obscenities.

"Everyone up against that wall!" one of them ordered in a heavy Brooklyn accent. "And *you*!" He pointed directly at Donovan. "Hand over the map."

2

"I had been hoping that we... that the country was finally about to put Vietnam behind us."

Hal Brognola stared at the President, who stood before the vast windows of the Oval Office, overlooking the Washington Monument. He turned slightly off to the right, and stared toward the black gash of a granite scar that he knew cut across the sprawling grounds that were the heart of the nation's capital.

Brognola watched the President gaze through the endless snowfall, toward the Vietnam War Memorial and the fifty-eight thousand etched names sparkling under warm display lamps, both beckoning and warning him, it seemed—warning them both. A trickle of words filled Brognola's head: *Thousand points of light...* He wondered if the President was thinking the same thing.

"We cannot allow those documents to get into the wrong hands," the President repeated.

"Yes, sir. I understand. Fully." Brognola chomped on his unlit Honduran cigar thoughtfully as he reflected on the afternoon's events: the red phone had rung at a few minutes past high noon. From Able Team's secluded headquarters at Stony Man Farm in Virginia's Shenandoah Valley, he'd had Jack Grimaldi whisk him over the Blue Ridge Mountains and down into Washington in record time. His presence was rarely requested at the White House.

Brognola was the director of Stony Man Farm. In that capacity he was known as the Chief, to the men of Able Team and Phoenix Force. Official liaison to the White House and various intelligence agencies and organizations based in the capital, he was a big gray-haired man with thick brows and a pronounced jaw. The jaw was always set firm—always ready for a confrontation—and his unequalled experience in urban concrete jungles and rain forest free-fire zones the world over had added perhaps a dozen years to his rough, no-nonsense appearance.

"You're familiar with Admiral Kruger?" the President now asked.

"Of course, sir," Brognola quickly responded. Kruger had been an OSS officer back in 1950s Indochina—the Office of Strategic Services being the predecessor of the CIA—and he was now one of the U.S. Armed Forces' highest-ranking Naval Intelligence officers.

"And the State Department has already filled you in on the scuttlebutt regarding the ten million in rubies or sapphires or something smuggled in from Saigon?"

"Emeralds, sir," Brognola said, shifting his weight from foot to foot, but not nervously. "Yes, sir."

"Yes, well...this emerald business appears to correspond with the recent defection in the Communist Vietnam regime. You know about the shake-up in Hanoi?"

"Yes, sir." It was already old news: a leading politician had defected, apparently taking with him a cache of long-missing gems and some prized documents, as well. Classified documents.

"American credibility could be damaged, the country's reputation tarnished, if the documents are located by the wrong agents, Hal."

"Yes, sir. Of course..."

The Vietnamese had already proposed a swap—the documents could cause problems between Hanoi and Moscow, as well. A swap. Traitor for traitor, spy for spy, double agent for double agent. *If* the defector could be located and apprehended.

Brognola knew the routine: he was a yes man, one of the last old soldiers. The President would give him a mission, and he would carry it out, no questions asked. He would recover the documents, or perish trying. And he'd never read their contents, or inquire as to what his people had just risked their skins for.

"Seven men were involved in the jewel caper, Hal," the President continued. "They smuggled the emeralds from Dien Bien Phu, south to Saigon, then north again to Hanoi. One of the 'Cult of Seven' is this recent defector—Tran Van Thieu. The defector made his move during an official visit to a SEATO conference in Singapore. He carried the jewels and documents in his diplomatic courier bags, best we can make out. He, of course, had immunity from customs search. It's too bad the Vietnamese didn't check him out when he was leaving Hanoi in the first place."

"They must have really trusted him. Or else he was powerful."

"In actuality he was a patriot working with the OSS prior to the 1954 Geneva accords, but chose, for personal reasons, to flee north to Hanoi afterward—after Vietnam was divided into North and South at the Seventeenth Parallel. Information has reached me via the State Department that clues to the exact location of the gems were hidden by this Cult of Seven at fourteen places throughout the world."

"But, sir," Brognola began, nervously clearing his throat. "If you don't mind..."

"You're curious as to why the Office of the President is involved in a case of missing emeralds that might not even exist when there are more pressing global matters at stake, right? It's because of the documents."

"Sir?"

"The documents are with the emeralds, Hal. Find one, you've got the other. And *we* want *the other* returned. As soon as possible. Am I making myself clear, or would you like someone to translate my orders into Thai for you?" That was a presidential joke. The Head of State was aware Brognola was attending Thai language classes at night—part of his constant training to increase his working knowledge of several different tongues.

"Admiral Kruger is coordinating all intelligence obtained on this matter to date," the President continued. "One of his men will be delivering a packet to Stony Man Farm within twenty-four hours."

"Yes, sir."

"We're still not sure how Tran got into the States—the Company thinks via Managua and the Mexican border."

"It would be easy enough," Brognola said, scratching at the stubble on his chin.

"I *want* those documents on my desk within seven days, Hal," the President insisted. "That's the deadline."

"Sir?"

"That's the longest I can hope to keep the media out of this mess."

"I understand, sir."

Brognola didn't have to ask about the contents of the documents because he already had some inkling about them—from Carl Lyons, who had already been briefed by both the CIA and NSA.

Carl Lyons was also a member of Able Team. He was a California native but knew little of the good life. Wearing the LAPD badge had taught him about good and evil, life and death. Two tours as a college football lineman were his first introduction to pain. His share of bullet wounds over the ensuing years enhanced his roughneck's résumé.

The agents whom Lyons had spoken with regarding the emeralds revealed that the documents were proof that a U.S.-sanctioned death squad had accidentally killed an important ally, a resistance leader in the 1950s. The official line had always been that the man had been killed in an accidental plane crash, his body never recovered.

"I cannot stress how important it is that this mission remain a strictly off-the-record affair," the President continued, bringing Brognola back to the present. "I'd love to bring in Delta Force, but there can be no use of any official Armed Forces unit right now, no matter how elite."

"Yes, sir. I understand."

The briefing was practically over now. But Brognola made no move to leave, nor did the President suggest he attend to other matters. There had to be something else on the President's mind. There had to be more to this mission than the recovery of some documents that were now more than thirty years old. After all, it was doubtful anyone cared about what had transpired in Indochina during the fifties—even the accidental murder of a beloved freedom fighter. And why wasn't the President's usual entourage of advisers present at the meeting?

Hal Brognola's head began to swim as a collage of thoughts pestered him: was the President somehow personally involved in all of this? Could he have perhaps been working for Admiral Kruger's death squads during the fifties? Or vice versa? Could the President have actually been the triggerman?

GADGETS SCHWARZ SLOWLY REACHED for the customized .45 automatic holstered beneath his black jean jacket, but hesitated when Peter K. Nunn fixed a cautionary gaze on both of the Club's guests. Big Don Donovan had just surrendered the jewel box to the shotgun-toting masked men, but didn't seem all that concerned as the bandits backed toward one of the exits.

"Don't no one make no funny moves!" one of the robbers threatened. His harsh Brooklyn accent seemed to make Donovan's smile grow.

"Recognize him?" Nunn whispered low but audibly.

"Yeah," Donovan said, nodding. "Worst Brooklyn accent I ever *hoid*."

"Imposters?"

"Yeah. Franklin and Dodge, I'd say. New *Joisy* chapter."

"That'd be my guess, too."

Blancanales moved his head slightly closer to the two reputed mercenaries. "What the hell's going on?"

"They're from the Adventurers Club out in Jersey," Donovan explained under his breath. "They'll go to any length to play a joke on us."

"And they use guns?" Schwarz's look of disapproval was obvious.

Neither Nunn nor Big Don Donovan were able to answer immediately, since a woman's scream, or war cry, interrupted the hushed verbal exchange.

Swinging a baseball bat she'd found leaning against the wall, Joan Andrews ran toward the two men. She knocked one of the Remingtons from the nearest gunman. His accomplice, however, aimed his own 12-gauge at her head and promptly pulled the trigger.

A weak fountain of water spurted from the barrel, striking Andrews in the face. She swung her bat again, missing her assailant's nose by inches.

Meanwhile, an indignant howl went up from the men clustered around the bar. And they charged—Big Don and Peter K. and a dozen other lesser-known hooligans.

Remaining on their bar stools, Schwarz and Blancanales watched the two gunmen disappear beneath a pile of flailing arms and legs as the soldiers of misfortune converged on them.

Five minutes later the emerald-hunting competitors from New Jersey's faction of the Adventurers Club sat atop the white marble table, back to back—their arms bound behind them.

"They never would have found it," Donovan said as he lifted the jewelry box between Gadgets and Politician. He tapped one of the intricately carved dragon heads along the contraption's edge, opening a secret panel along the false bottom.

"But what about those?" Schwarz asked, pointing to the roll of parchmentlike papers.

"Aw, I ripped 'em out of a comic book last week," Donovan admitted as he carefully withdrew a cracked and yellowing sliver of carbonlike paper from the secret compartment. "With them New *Joisy* clowns so close, it's always kind of like the Boy Scouts around here. You know, 'Be prepared.'"

"You didn't expect us to have the actual *map*, did you?" Nunn blustered.

Donovan held the carbon up to the slowly twirling Chinese lantern. "But we've got one of the carbons the Indochinese pirates used when they were drawin' up the hiding places," he lied easily.

Schwarz laughed. "You expect us to believe that? They didn't even *use* carbon paper back then." He turned to Blancanales. "Did they, old man?"

Rosario frowned. "How the hell would *I* know?" he shot back. "But one thing I *do* know: this joint is fast becoming a bad joke I don't have time for. I'm heading back to the hotel. How about you?"

"*I* want to see the map," Gadgets insisted.

Frown deepening, Donovan nevertheless surrendered it without further argument.

Schwarz stared at the map for almost a minute before speaking. "Cong Ly. Le Van Duyet. Tu Do. Le Loi. It's a street map of Old Saigon. How's that going to help you? I thought you said the jewels had been moved to the U.S., Big Don."

"They have. It won't." Dejected, Donovan folded the tattered map back up and replaced it in the jewelry box's false bottom. "You know how it is. We've been planning this caper for a couple of years now: going back to Vietnam, sneaking into Saigon, retrieving the jewels..."

"Impossible," Schwarz argued. "Even if you were all Asian, you'd never get past the Vietnamese police. No way."

"Yeah, you're probably right. But old men need a dream, don't they?" Donovan allowed a slight gleam to sparkle in his narrowed eyes for an instant.

"The damn jewels probably don't even exist," Nunn muttered.

All eyes shifted to the lounge's main entrance as a tall, stocky man clad in various shades of black entered the Adventurers Club. "Ironman..." Blancanales announced under his breath.

"I've been looking for you two clowns all over the Big Apple," Carl Lyons growled, seeming to ignore everyone else in the suddenly silent bar, yet missing nothing, no one. "You weren't at any of the usual haunts."

"That damn Cowboy," Gadgets grumbled, referring to Cowboy Kissinger, the Farm's resident weaponsmith, who also made every attempt humanly possible to maintain close tabs on the men working for Hal Brognola. "I *told* him where we'd be."

Lyons ignored the excuse. It was all part of the plan, the cover. The club had, in reality, been his first and only stop tonight. Ironman's ice-blue eyes shifted to Donovan—who he vaguely recognized—then to Nunn, who glanced away. "I'm afraid duty calls, gentlemen. Say goodbye to your friends." His eyes darted to the bartender's cold, unimpressed orbs. "Do they owe anything?"

"Nope," Glenn said, nodding solemnly as he continued polishing his empty beer mugs.

"Then let's go," Lyons said, wrapping an arm around his two comrades and guiding them toward the exits. But not before his eyes locked with those belonging to Joan Andrews. There was a faint gleam of recognition in his eyes and

Joan, in her own way, smiled back. The exchange went unnoticed by the other grim-faced patrons.

"Yeah," she said cryptically as Able Team sauntered out the door. "That's what I thought."

"What's it all about?"

Lyons stared back at Gadgets Schwarz. "I just heard from Brognola."

"So, what are the real details of this mission?" Schwarz asked, cracking his knuckles loudly. "I've been itching for some action."

"That's the spirit," Lyons said, smiling for the first time. "But actually we'll probably be dancing toe to toe with Buddhists on this one. Before leaving Stony Man we met with Admiral Kruger."

"That spooky tunes senior sailor with the owl's eyebrows?" Blancanales snickered.

Lyons's tight grin faded. "I wouldn't underestimate him, Pol. Kruger's been offing enemies of Old Glory since before you and me graduated from diapers. Just because he's Navy doesn't mean he can't kick ass and take names with the best of us."

"I got nothing against the Navy," Blancanales, a former Black Beret, muttered. "After all, the SEALs are Navy, man, and in my book the SEALs are a notch above the Army's Special Forces."

"Now wait a minute," Schwarz started to protest, but Lyons cut them both off.

"This is no time for a sparring session," he said. "Kruger knows his shit. He may look like some absentminded professor, but he has double agents in every government from China to Colombia. Apparently all this noise about a recent transfer of jewels to some hiding place stateside is nothing more than a smoke screen. They've been in the U.S. for nearly twenty years now."

"They?"

"The emeralds, Gadgets! Remember the story the State Department officials told us? They were actually hidden back in the early seventies by an elderly member of this so-called Cult of Seven, an old guy known around Saigon as One-eyed Ngoc."

Lyons then told them about Tran Van Thieu, the defector, as well. "Brognola claims the President never mentioned One-eyed Ngoc. And he spoke about the emeralds as if they'd only recently left Asian soil."

"Meaning?" Blancanales asked, tilting his head to one side.

"I get the distinct impression the President doesn't know as much about this whole incident as Admiral Kruger does, that he's unaware the ten million in emeralds made it stateside as far back as 1970." He read the perplexed look in their eyes. "The documents? Well, that's another matter entirely."

Blancanales and Schwarz exchanged glances as they reflected on the primary topic of conversation that had taken place back at the Adventurers Club. "Just what exactly do Brognola and the President want us to do?" Gadgets asked.

"Locate Tran Van Thieu and One-eyed Ngoc sooner than ASAP, gentlemen. And confiscate those damn documents."

"What about the ten million in emeralds?" Blancanales asked, producing an odd smile.

"Yeah." Schwarz's chin rose slightly. "What do we do with *them*? Turn 'em into customs or something?" His tone told the others he thought that such an action would just be a waste of good jewels.

"The Boss said nothing about the emeralds. The impression I got was that whoever recovered them . . . well, what's the old saying? 'Losers weepers, finders keepers.'"

"That doesn't sound like the Hal *I* know," Blancanales said. His grin became a frown of suspicion.

"Consider 'em a sort of...addition to your pension fund," Lyons quipped.

Schwarz laughed bitterly. "What pension fund?"

"Look," Lyons sighed, then took in a deep breath to show he was tiring of all the talk. "The important thing is that the emeralds will lead us to the documents, or vice versa. Let's just get out there and recover the classified papers, okay, guys? Or your next job—*our* next job—just might include sloshing through the muck in some god-forsaken Vietnamese rice paddy."

Schwarz and Blancanales both knew that Lyons's comment was a play on words—black humor involving the old cynical in-country GI adage, "What can they do—send me to Vietnam?"

But none of the Able Team commandos were laughing.

3

One-eyed Ngoc stared out the grimy window of his seventh-floor flat in San Francisco's Chinatown. Below, the busy intersection of Stockton and Bush Streets was clogged with delivery trucks and taxis competing to get through the bumper-to-bumper congestion. Someone had accidentally knocked down the traffic lights pole. The sound of a cop's shrill whistle reached his ears.

Only a couple of miles to the east, San Francisco Bay and the World Trade Center Building merged the ice-blue sea with an impressive silver skyline, but One-eyed Ngoc could see none of this. His view was obstructed by a long line of high-rise sweatshops that made up this part of the garment district.

Ngoc's room was located in a nondescript tenement that was one of dozens of such cinder-block housing projects in San Francisco's Chinatown. But, unlike a majority of his fellow tenants, Ngoc didn't pay the rent with government assistance. Although he had no outwardly visible means of support, Ngoc had his own personal checking account in the Far East New China Savings and Loan down on Mason Street, a short, brisk walk from the Cable Car Museum located off Washington. Monthly allotments were deposited in the account by the Crimson Serpent Import-Export Company located in the huge Embarcadero Center complex. The Crimson Serpent was a front for the Vietnamese Secret Police and handled all accounts in the continental U.S. It coordinated all Vietnamese espionage activities stateside, as well.

But Ngoc had lately become quite tense. The deposit for the previous month had failed to materialize—as had the funds he'd been expecting the day before. Something was wrong. His urgent cables to Tran Van Thieu—via the Viet consulate in New York City—had gone unanswered. Tran had always responded; he was Ngoc's field supervisor. Ngoc's first thought was that Tran had actually defected.

The thought made Ngoc chuckle. He usually met Tran at the Chrysanthemum Café on Clay Street in the heart of Chinatown—about once every two weeks—where they exchanged the latest gossip, but little more. The Vietnamese government had few tasks for Ngoc to do these days. In actuality Hanoi held no trust for the old man anymore. Not since rumors began circulating that he had had a part in the theft, some two decades earlier, of a large quantity of precious stones from Vietnamese soil. The Communist regime frowned on extracurricular activities by its agents—especially if such hobbies enriched those agents.

The two men now did little more than sip ginseng tea. Ngoc would brag about the young girl he was going to purchase for a night's services when the next allotment check arrived. And Tran would spend his time complaining about the bureaucracy in Hanoi, and how they should break the ancient pact and simply divide up the emeralds and disappear into the Asian underground. That always elicited another laugh, of course. The Vietnamese Secret Police would find them, sooner or later. The vacation would quickly come to an unceremonious end.

No, they needed to obtain something else before betraying the government that had become the ultimate traitor to its people. They would need some sort of insurance—a safety valve. Possessing sensitive information wasn't good enough. Tran could easily obtain it with his high position in the regime, but even classified data and highest-order secrets were time-sensitive. No, they would need something more valuable to use against the government. One-eyed Ngoc wondered if Tran Van Thieu had finally discovered that special something and, in finding it, elected to permanently flee their homeland for the easy life in America.

Something was certainly up. No surreptitious bank deposit via the consulate, and no word from Tran. Ngoc knew he had to move the scroll. He could sense that there was a dangerous situation unfolding. Agents from Hanoi might actually be closing in on his apartment at that very moment.

It was time to move.

Ngoc focused his stare on the brilliant arcs of heat lightning crackling along the northern horizon. Thunder rolled down through San Francisco Bay.

Fearing that the rattling of the windowpanes might be an ominous warning, he rushed over to the kitchen sink on the other side of the apartment, climbed up onto the counter and carefully drew the bamboo curtains and the cloth shutter behind them.

The door to his apartment had two dead bolts aside from the regular doorknob lock and safety latch, but Ngoc still found himself glancing back over his shoulder before he removed the small wooden panel connecting the kitchen ceiling to the apartment's west wall. A brown wire cord appeared, and he gently pulled on this until a plastic tube one inch in diameter and roughly ten inches long protruded from its dark place of concealment.

Ngoc grinned. Not very fancy, but effective. His enemies would have to tear the entire apartment apart before they'd find the tiny crevice lined with putty and plastic wood. Ngoc paused as the thunder—closer now—shook the red roof tiles overhead. He listened intently to the first sheet of falling raindrops, wondering just who his enemies were. And how he would identify them.

There had always been someone scheming to steal what was rightly his, what belonged to his friends in Mot Bo Bay—the Cult of Seven.

Ngoc didn't bother replacing the slender strip of paneling. He opened the plastic tube's end plug and removed a cracked and yellowing sliver of parchment the size of a college diploma. He quickly inspected the information scribbled across it in red ink—just in case. His enemies could be very clever. But the fourteen addresses and locations listed by state were the correct ones, and he replaced the scroll.

Ngoc was under no false illusions, however. He was well aware that possessing the List of Fourteen brought him no closer to the emeralds. Hidden at each location was a further clue to the jewel cache's exact whereabouts—none of which, individually, did the seeker any good. The clues could only be used in combination, and exactly how even Ngoc was still not quite sure, despite the passage of all these years.

It was the General who had insisted on creating the List of Fourteen, of always maintaining a written record of the emeralds' exact hiding place. "We are all getting older and wiser, but not necessarily craftier," the General had maintained at their last clandestine meeting in Old Saigon before the fall of South Vietnam. "In fact, we may, before long, begin experiencing the subtle erosion of a few of our mental faculties, gentlemen. Therefore, a permanent record of some sort should be scrupulously maintained."

"If we're all about to go senile," Ngoc had countered sarcastically, "the better to split up the goods now while we can still enjoy their benefits."

Tran and the General had both laughed. "In time," the General had said. "All in good time, Ngoc."

"When the time is *right*," Tran Van Thieu had added cryptically.

Although he was sometimes suspicious of Tran's motivations, Ngoc had never doubted the General's sincerity and trustworthiness. It was well known that the General's family was extremely wealthy, had been, in fact, for the past twelve generations. Rumor had it that their riches rivaled those of the emperor's domain at the Imperial City of Hue. Though he could have led a pampered life from birth, the General had taken to military pursuits in his mid-twenties, quickly rising in rank until he became a field commander in the Army of the Republic of Vietnam. When the South fell to the North in 1975, he became head of the Tu Do Luc Quan faction of the Resistance, in absentia, although it was rumored he often ventured back into the homeland via Nong Kai, Thailand's Mekong River junction with the Laotian border. And now it seemed that the General had deserted Ngoc. The General and Tran Van Thieu.

"Perhaps the General is busy killing the 'Communist barbarians,'" Ngoc muttered under his breath as he carefully pocketed the plastic tube, peered out the peephole and finally left his apartment. "But Tran? Ah, what of my old friend Tran Van Thieu?"

It was funny how fate altered both attitude and ideology, Ngoc decided. The General had no idea Ngoc and Tran were Communist agents and had been since the three men were young adults, content at chasing raven-haired maidens from the Central Highlands to the Mekong Delta.

They could have blown the General's cover fourteen years ago, when Saigon first fell, but Tran and Ngoc and their VC cronies were patient. There was no hurry. Things in the Orient—lives and deaths and destiny—had an odd way of running in cycles.

One-eyed Ngoc was a stooped man who appeared to be in his late fifties or early sixties. He wore a black patch over the left socket where his eyeball had been plucked out during a seafaring accident forty years earlier when he was a deckhand with the Binh Xuyen river pirates—forerunners of the Saigon police. He wore baggy black pantaloons, a gray T-shirt and thongs. Just another half-blind Chinaman ambling down the side street—at least that was the image he hoped to portray once he reached the ground floor, seven flights down. The elevator in Ngoc's building wasn't working again this week. He wheezed as he hobbled down the concrete steps, clinging to the railing. Returning—laboring *up* the seven flights—was what he detested most. But one adjusted to life's little tests.

At the foot of the stairs Ngoc noticed a shoeshine boy crouching on the bottom step. The youth was Chinese—he spoke with a Taiwanese accent—and was probably no older than ten or eleven. But the two of them exchanged bold winks when One-eyed Ngoc passed, as if they'd been scheming and planning and executing cheap heists together for decades.

"Good kid," Ngoc muttered under his breath in Vietnamese as soon as he was out of earshot. He paid the boy a dollar a day to let him know if any strangers entered the tenement—especially *gwai-loh* or Caucasians. Even seven flights to the top floor, sound carried easily up and down the doorless stairwell. Five rings on the boy's bicycle bell meant, "Strangers in the building." Six rings, "Police." Seven, "Disregard." Even with his door closed, Ngoc could easily hear the youth's signals when they came. The walls were as thin as tissue paper, it often seemed.

As Ngoc scurried off down the sidewalk toward the intersection with Bush Street, he glanced over his shoulder several times, but no one seemed to be following him.

It took the Oriental less than ten minutes to reach one of the many concrete stairwells leading down to the underground subway system. Once safely below the street, he ignored the signs pointing the way to ticket booths and turnstiles and hurried off in the opposite direction until he came upon several orange barricades in a barely lit area.

Finally, beyond a No Admittance ribbon, he entered an old construction zone and disappeared down a section of dark tunnel that had long ago been abandoned by the San

Francisco Subway Projects Commission. It was too hazardous, the developers had claimed. Natural gas had leaked up through the core samples, and several consulting geologists were of the opinion that an immense underground bed of seawater lay just beyond the brittle wall of sedimentary rocks that had supported the project to this point.

One-eyed Ngoc waited in the shadows for nearly ten minutes to ensure, once again, that he hadn't been trailed. Then the former river pirate darted off down a narrow passageway until he came to a dead-end wall of bricks. Hastily he piled several nearby cinder blocks against the wall, then climbed up and dislodged a loose brick seven or eight feet above the floor.

From behind the brick Ngoc removed an old snub-nosed revolver, stuffed it down into his trousers and then carefully inserted the plastic tube into the cavity before replacing the brick. He slapped it with the palm of his hand several times, ensuring a tight fit, then—suddenly showing unusual agility for a man of his age and stature—hustled back toward the section of subway tunnel being used by the general public.

Within ten minutes he was back at his apartment building, a few beads of sweat on his brow, but his breathing actually quite normal. On the way up the stairwell he again nodded to the young boy, who was still sitting on his shoeshine box, now absorbed in a comic book called *Nam*.

One-eyed Ngoc knew that many *gwai-loh* kids these days spent their free time reading fictionalized accounts about what the old Asian hands called Vietnam War I. The Resistance advocates claimed Vietnam War II would soon be waged by the freedom fighters and that, in due course, all Vietnamese citizens desiring to return to their homeland would be able to do so.

Ngoc didn't think he would live to see that day. Besides, he was becoming complacent in Chinatown and was comfortable with his new life-style. Thought of the emeralds—

ten million dollars worth of sparkling green gems—was the only thing that kept Ngoc motivated. Money was everything. Money purchased sexual pleasures. Politics no longer mattered.

Sipping his tea back in the deceptive safety of his quiet parlor, Ngoc gazed at his prized collection of research archives—ancient tomes from across the world, but particularly the Orient. Money also purchased his books.

Someone knocked at his door and, still thinking about which volume to bring down off the floor-to-ceiling bookshelves, Ngoc abandoned his earlier caution and casually opened the dead bolts. After all, the prize was safe now, several blocks away.

Jaw dropping, his eyes flew wide as two armed men charged in, knocking him to the floor.

ON THE STAIRWELL landing below, ten-year-old Vincent Lu—who had been named for his mother's favorite American actor, Vincent Price—closed his comic book and cocked an ear. Vincent had been weaned on Price horror films and, although he considered himself an expert on Hollywood shock tactics and was able to weather even the most terrifying plot twists or unexpected screen developments, Lu was unable to mask his growing fear.

There was no mistaking the stifled cry above—it had come from Old Man Ngoc. Had he fallen? Or… No. Young Vincent Lu could definitely hear the sounds of a scuffle taking place far overhead, and he began running up the stairwell, wondering who was beating on Old Man Ngoc, and how had they gotten past his ground-floor post?

When he reached the point midway between the sixth and seventh floors, Vincent Lu heard a wicked scream. In his mind he envisioned a long dagger being plunged into Old Man Ngoc's heart—not unlike the bayonet charges colorfully depicted in the last several issues of his favorite comic.

Frozen with sudden, unexpected terror—hadn't he witnessed crime after crime being committed in Chinatown since arriving from a Hong Kong refugee camp four years ago, and been hardened to life on the streets?—Lu clung to the iron railing, praying that the attackers of Old Man Ngoc didn't flee down this stairwell, but left the same way they entered.

"Thank you," Vincent Lu whispered under his breath as he heard the fire escape outside One-eyed Ngoc's balcony rattle as the old man's assailants hurriedly left by that route.

Vincent waited nearly a minute, huddled there in the stairwell's protective darkness, before curiosity forced him to venture out onto the seventh floor. Old Man Ngoc's door was wide open. Down the hallway a woman peered out of her apartment, eyes locking briefly with Vincent's, before she slammed the door shut. He could hear the muffled voices of other tenants, too scared to unbolt their own doors and investigate.

In cautious silence—practicing the stealth and cunning of his comic book heroes—Vincent slowly approached the open doorway. A bloody trail was all that was left behind in the abandoned flat. No intruders. No discarded weapons or misplaced loot. Just a trail leading through the living room toward the balcony.

Whoever the mysterious attackers had been, they had taken One-eyed Ngoc along with them when they left.

CARL LYONS WAS PREPARING to enjoy an afternoon cup of Vietnamese coffee at an open-air café on Clay Street. The rain had forced him to order his lunch inside the enclosed veranda. Huge plate-glass windows took up most of the walls throughout this portion of the restaurant. Heavy raindrops pelted the tinted skylights overhead.

Pol Blancanales had introduced him to the powerful Vietnamese brew several years back—its potent caffeine jolt was many times stronger than even the best espresso. And with the bottom layer of sweet French cream that came with every cup, the mixture was gentle on the stomach.

After adding several mint leaves and a drop or two of lemon juice to the bean sprouts in his accompanying bowl of noodle soup, Ironman prepared to dig in. And then he noticed a blue uniform approaching.

The uniform had shapely curves that even the unflattering body armor couldn't conceal. Lyons's eye shifted from the San Francisco Police patch to the woman's blond hair, which she had tried unsuccessfully to pile up into a bun under her patrol cap.

Wiping the rainwater from the brim of her cap, her eyes scanned the dozen or so customers at the café, then came to rest on Lyons and wavered. It was obvious that she sensed something different in this man and it wasn't just that he was Caucasian, while everyone else at the Chrysanthemum Café was Asian. There was something in the way he sat: back to the wall, wary eyes narrowed as they inspected all who approached, even her. She knew the look. Only ex-cons and cops had it. After exchanging nods, she walked on toward the rest room at the back of the café.

Shortly after she disappeared behind a bamboo bead partition, four Chinese youths walked in through a swinging set of double doors on the other side of the restaurant. Lyons recognized their overconfident gait immediately—the look of pent-up anger in their eyes, the defiance in their raised chins, the bulges under their sport jackets.

Their jackets were expensive, flashy, but worn over faded jeans and scuffed shoes. Soaked from the rainfall outside, they were in their early twenties, with long, slicked-back hair and a proliferation of gold necklaces. It was obvious: these men weren't customers.

Lyons glanced toward the rest room. Then he looked back at the gang of hoodlums as their ringleader leaned across a cash register and grabbed the front of the proprietor's shirt. Lyons heard silk ripping.

"You're late, old bastard!" the thug hissed. "No more slack! No more warnings!"

A few heads turned at the verbal disturbance, only to resume manipulating chopsticks or hiding behind newspapers when met with glares from the extortionists.

Lyons glanced toward the rest room again. "Where the hell is she?" he grumbled softly to himself. His gun hand slowly slid under his jacket, feeling the reassuring cold steel of his own holstered weapon. Lyons was torn between rushing off to warn the policewoman, and just sitting back, lying low, waiting to see how she handled herself, offering his own sharpshooter's services only as a last resort.

This was no time for chauvinistic games, though, a tiny voice of warning echoed in his head. He'd seen Asian gangbangers at work in the past. They seldom played by the rules, and were more apt to start shooting wildly at the first appearance of a badge.

"Damn," he muttered, slowly taking a long gulp from the half-filled glass of steaming liquid. He set the coffee down, drew his pistol and was starting to rise when the officer emerged from the rest room.

Smiling as she locked eyes with him again, her eyes shifted to the confrontation at the cash register and, immediately assessing the situation, the smile vanished. She drew her .38 Special and, holding the four-inch revolver down against her thigh, barrel pointed at the grimy tiles, she advanced toward the group of punks, totally ignoring Ironman now.

As she strode past, he focused on her name tag: Klein. Out of the corner of his eye, Lyons saw the Asians drawing their guns, prepared to risk brutal death by hot lead and hollowpoints rather than submit to a simple roust. Lyons knew that every last one of them probably had felony warrants out for their arrests.

Sighing, he too drew his pistol and, momentarily, Officer Klein's face registered terror as she detected the move in her peripheral vision. Her confidence at confronting some of the local underworld denizens eroded instantly.

But there was no time now for her to further assess the situation, or determine the big man's intent. The gang leader had released the café owner's shirt and pushed the old man back over a chair. Right fist flying out, his fingers were curled around a chrome-plated revolver. Without saying a word to his fellow vermin, the gangster began unloading on the policewoman with six deafening Magnum discharges, one after the other.

Screaming, several patrons scattered. A table was up-ended in Lyons's path. He kicked it aside, Colt Python extended at arm's length now as the hood's barrage of flying lead passed between Ironman and the officer, shattering a plate-glass window behind them. One of the rounds wounded a schoolgirl passing by on the sidewalk outside, and a ricochet struck a school bus inching down the crowded street.

Pandemonium broke out as the yellow bus slammed into the back of a delivery truck carrying butane tanks. Several explosions shook the walls of buildings rising up on all four sides.

The policewoman dropped into a crouch as more windows were blown inward and fireballs rose toward the roof-tops outside.

Lyons had never taken his eyes off the extortionists and, as their eyes drifted toward the confusion taking place outside, Ironman cocked his eight-inch revolver's hammer back on single action and gently, expertly squeezed off a quick-kill shot that sent a thunderous .357 slug through the gunman's forehead, instantly severing the nerve wires connecting brain to limbs. The Asian's pistol clattered to the floor an instant before his lifeless body dropped onto a folding metal chair.

The chair collapsed loudly and, gun hand shifting, Lyons pointed the Python's front sight at the nearest gang member, allowing his own reflexes to guide the next round. When his eyes locked onto another weapon being drawn, he brought in the trigger again, this time twice.

A second body collapsed across the soiled tiles.

Lyons, too, finally dropped into a defensive crouch as he shifted to take on the other young gangsters, but one of the Asians was already firing.

He heard the earsplitting crack and hiss, snakelike, as a .45-caliber slug missed his earlobe by inches. Lyons fired off three rounds in rapid succession at the thug. He knew that all three struck the upper torso. He was also well aware he was running on empty and that there was still one more armed punk out there, twenty yards away, kneeling behind the cash register.

Bringing out his speedloader, Lyons dropped to one knee and flipped open the Python's cylinder as the gangster finally began shooting wildly. With blinding speed, Ironman ejected the empty shell casings from his Colt and slammed home fresh cartridges.

His attention was distracted by the policewoman's blood-spattered cap bouncing off the floor in front of his knee.

4

"Is that him?"

"How am I supposed to know?"

"Well, does he look like the Viet in the file photo?"

Gadgets Schwarz stared down at the glossy black-and-white for a moment. He glanced out through the van's tinted window at the slender Asian exiting the four-story brownstone office building in midtown Manhattan, then back down at the photo again. "Could be. But maybe not."

"Give me those!" Blancanales ordered as he grabbed Schwarz's folding binoculars. Swiftly he zoomed in on the fifty-year-old wearing a gray pin-striped three-piece suit. "Yeah, it's him."

"How do *you* know?" Schwarz asked, sounding skeptical. "We're not close enough to actually—"

"The scar, amigo. He's got the claw-shaped scar on his chin." Blancanales was already climbing forward between the two front seats. "Let's do it, buster."

They waited for Tran Van Thieu to cross the street through a break in traffic, then slowly coasted down the block as he approached the parking lot where his black Mercedes was strategically situated near the front exit.

"Why don't we take him now?" Gadgets asked.

"As soon as he unlocks the car door." Blancanales's jaw was set firmly as he eyeballed the setting sun—its crimson glory was even causing Tran to gaze at the western horizon in awe.

"As soon as he unlocks the door? Ain't that pushing it?" Schwarz shook his head from side to side.

"I want to see what he's got inside the coupe," Blanca-nales said simply.

"We can—"

"You ever try breaking into a Mercedes?" Rosario asked, anticipating his partner's suggestion. But he anticipated wrong.

"Once we nab the sucker we'll have his car keys, too, Pol. But if we cut it too close, he might jump in and burn rub-ber on us before we can get to him."

"You're right," Blancanales agreed, altering his plan and gunning the gas pedal without warning. He drove up be-tween Tran and his Mercedes with such dramatics that the wide-eyed Vietnamese, fearing he was about to be run down, threw up his hands in fright. Politician was still talking as he rammed the gearshift into Park. "I was thinkin' about the sunset and how much more glorious it's gonna look after this mission's over and yours truly is sucking down mai-tais on some white sand beach in Tahiti or Penang or—"

But Schwarz was no longer listening to Pol's tireless ti-rade. Instead, he was already bolting out the van's side door, barreling toward the target in a fast sprint.

Detaining Tran was easier than both of the Able Team commandos had anticipated. He was unarmed and offered no resistance whatsoever. However, once it became clear to the Communist agent that this wasn't a street assassination as he had originally feared, the questions began rapidly flying forth. "What is this?" he demanded. "Who are you? Why are you—"

Grabbing a wrist, Schwarz twirled Tran Van Thieu around and slammed him up against the van for a cursory frisk. The Vietnamese was carrying only his wallet and keys. "Shut up," Gadgets replied calmly.

"Is this a robbery?" Tran continued. "Were you two thugs sent by—"

"Knock it off!" Blancanales ordered as he jabbed a Colt 45 automatic into the small of Tran's back as his eyes scanned passing traffic for any approaching police officers. The three of them stood behind the van—between it and the Mercedes—and, for the most part, the confrontation went unnoticed. Schwarz glanced over at the parking lot attendant. He was reclining on a swivel chair inside a glass booth, feet propped on the cash register, his back to them as he watched the evening news on a small portable TV set.

"Let's go!" Blancanales directed after Schwarz had securely tied Tran's hands behind his back with fiberglass flexicuffs.

"Where to?" Tran asked, baring his teeth threateningly now. He was a small man—about five foot two and barely a hundred and twenty-five pounds—but wiry and agile, with firmly toned limbs and no paunch. His thick jet-black hair had a few streaks of gray and was close-cropped on the sides, but bushy on top and combed forward. It was the old NVA style favored by North Vietnamese regulars, Blancanales noted. "I *demand* to know where you're taking me!"

"To a one-on-one with Uncle Sammy," Blancanales sneered, his eyes probing Tran's in a taunting, threatening manner. Uncle Sammy was an old GI term back in the war, used to indicate any body of government associated with the Army's Green Machine, the U.S. embassy or the Pentagon.

"I demand to speak with a representative of—" Tran sputtered. "I demand to be taken to—"

"You ain't in much of a position to demand anything." Schwarz's laugh was forced and coated with equal tension. Gadgets roughly guided Tran over to the van's side and hurled him inside. "This here's an *un*official act of sanctioned kidnapping and—"

"You're CIA!" Tran said, lifting his nose in the air defiantly. "I knew it! You're U.S. State Department and—"

"We ain't Agency spooks." Schwarz was beginning to enjoy the verbal exchange slightly as he handed Tran's car keys to Politician, then climbed in behind Tran.

"I've got friends in the Company, you know!" Tran boasted. "I know some G-Men, too!"

"And we ain't FBI, or even CID. We're so ultrasecret and blatantly rogue," Gadgets began, licking his lips provocatively, "that we could cut off your head and deposit it on the State Department's doorstep and there'd *still* be no repercussions, Thieu-baby."

Through the tinted windows they both watched Blancanales give the Mercedes a thorough search—trunk, glove compartment and floorboards.

Tran sat back against a wall of the van. "You're going to kill me?" he asked with a loud sigh of surrender. He stared out at the impressive silhouette of gray and silver skyscrapers that seemed to go on forever.

"Anything's possible," Schwarz answered, frowning as Blancanales started back toward the van, empty-handed.

"What is it you two want?" Tran asked, his eyes shifting to the gentle arc of the Brooklyn Bridge rising up through the mists of twilight. He wondered if it just might be the last thing he ever saw before some blinding muzzle-flash snuffed out his life. Tran closed his eyes tightly, working on the flexicuffs. He had held his wrists slightly apart when the fiberglass strips were first slipped on. He jerked tightly, but a wave of nausea now swirled through him as he realized they were too tight to squeeze out of. The two gunmen had counteracted his move without saying anything snide— they'd simply pulled the strips so tight the circulation in his wrists was cut off. Tran wasn't dealing with the usual breed of hired street toughs. These two were pros. "What is it you want?" Tran repeated. "Is it money? Money from the highest bidder? If that's the case, then—"

"Hardly."

"I'll *double* whatever it is you're being paid to—"

The opening of the van's doors silenced Tran. "Clean," Blancanales reported as he leaned inside.

"Nothing?"

"That's what I said."

"The Chief said to check under the hood, too. And down in the gas tank tube and—"

"Hell, we could slice the tires and upholstery open, too, for all the good it would do," Blancanales said, shrugging. "Do I look like a border patrolman at some San Diego Immigration checkpoint, eager to strip-search that Mercedes? Why don't we just tow the sucker and—"

"Negative," Schwarz said firmly. "We leave the wheels here. The Chief was adamant about that."

"Well, maybe Ho Chi Minh here's got them back at his pad."

"He wouldn't be that stupid. The Chief's got a team headed over there right now, anyway. But—"

"Yeah," Blancanales said, nodding. "I agree. He wouldn't be that stupid." His eyes shifted to their prisoner's. "*Would* you, Mr. Tran?"

"Perhaps you two could just come right out and tell me what you're searching for?"

Lapsing into a tense silence, Schwarz and Blancanales exchanged annoyed looks as they decided what to do next. Finally Gadgets caressed the ventilated barrel and customized blue-steel suppressor on his 9 mm automatic. "The documents, Tran," he said softly. "We want the documents you brought out of Vietnam."

Tran laughed easily. He controlled himself, studied their faces intently for a moment, then erupted into more laughter that was unrestrained this time around.

"What's so funny?" Blancanales asked, irritation lacing his features.

"Are you sure you two wanted *me*?" Tran's eyes gleamed. "*This* Tran Van Thieu?"

Schwarz appeared slightly taken aback. "I assure you tha you're the only Tran Van Thieu on our shit list this week.'

"And are you two misfits aware that I officially defected this week? That I am no longer considered a Communis dupe, no longer a security risk? I am free to—"

"Yeah, yeah, we know all that!" Schwarz silenced hin with the wave of a hand. "Free to roam with the buffalo and sing 'Home on the Range.' But it's come to Uncle Sammy' attention that you fled Vietnam with more documents than you surrendered to the State Department, pal. You've go some secret shit stashed away somewhere in case of a rainy day, right? Well, Uncle Sammy wants to take a gander a those dossiers, and he wants to check 'em out now."

"Incredible," Tran said, shaking his head in resignation as he settled back against the wall of the van again. "I simply don't know *where* you people get your information."

"There are double agents on both sides, Tran," Blancanales said bitterly. "Someone must have turned on you."

"Well, whoever they are, they've deceived you and your government and whoever's really behind all this. I have nothing—no documents, other than the papers I turned over to your embassy people...the papers detailing Soviet naval operations at Cam Ranh Bay. Therefore—"

"Therefore, we're just going to have to subject you to a little session of truth-or-consequences," Blancanales said, grinning like a demon unleashed.

Tran Van Thieu didn't look worried or intimidated. "That was just what I was about to suggest," he said, smiling weakly. "You have no other choice."

AFTER SLAMMING THE PYTHON'S well-oiled cylinder shut, Lyons delivered four rapid-fire rounds into the counter on which the café's cash register sat. With a startled cry the gunman was thrown back out of hiding when the two slugs impacted against his sternum with bone-crushing force. His own pistol flew through the air, bouncing off the ceiling.

Ironman started to rise slowly as several terrified female faces on the other side of the restaurant peeked out at him from behind cover. Then he remembered Patrolwoman Klein. His eyes darted to her upended, blood-spattered PD-blue cap. Then he started to turn toward the spot where he'd last seen her.

"Not so fast, hotshot."

An ice-cold gun barrel was suddenly resting firmly against the back of his skull. "Now slowly... lower the gun or you head tomorrow's entries in the local obituaries."

He assumed it was the female officer talking—that somehow she had survived her wound or wounds. "Listen," he began softly, "you've got this all wrong. I'm one of the good guys, and I—"

"Drop the gun!" she shouted into his ear this time, ramming her own service weapon forward and leaving a bruise against the base of his skull.

"Okay, okay!" Lyons hastily complied. This wasn't Hollywood, however. He wasn't about to drop his gun. He had the utmost respect and love for firearms—paid good money for the eight-inch Python—and refused to simply drop it. The Colt carried a six-digit serial number and was one of the last handmade Pythons; the pistol was his pride and joy. Slowly he dropped into a crouch and laid the weapon on the floor.

"Now follow it down, sweet thing."

"What?"

"Get your butt down on the floor and spread-eagle!"

Lyons hesitated only a second. "It's grimy and sticky and coated with stale beer and—"

It was the wrong choice of words. The officer brought both of her palms down hard against his shoulder blades, somehow managing to knock Lyons flat. Her knee jabbed into the small of his back.

"Hey, easy," he protested softly.

"Shut up!" she directed with a gut-flopping mixture of confidence and fear.

"Yeah, and who was it that saved your life a couple of minutes ago, girl," Lyons replied sarcastically. *"You* didn't manage to drop the hammer on even *one* of those bastards."* In the distance he heard sirens. Dozens of them. The café owner had obviously called for reinforcements.

Klein fumbled with her handcuffs without holstering her service revolver, and the set of iron bracelets clattered onto the floor.

"Need any help back there?" Lyons asked with a smirk as he started to glance over his shoulder.

"You're either a cop or an ex-cop," she muttered, pushing his face forward again, finally snapping one half of the cuffs around his right wrist. Lyons didn't resist, though he was beginning to feel it would be no great trick to flip to the side, disarm the female officer and leave her wearing her own handcuffs.

He felt her slip the free cuff under his belt, then attach it to his other wrist. Not bad, he decided: dropping the cuffs initially, then utilizing the Academy procedure of applying them, told him she was either a rookie or extremely nervous—possibly because this was her first shooting situation. "Only cops or ex-cops talk like that," she repeated.

"Maybe I'm a Mafia hit man." Lyons laughed grimly as several black-and-whites began skidding up outside. From the corner of one eye he managed to see two patrolmen advance, nightsticks in hand, and he groaned inwardly, hoping these guys were professional enough to show some restraint.

Officers wearing flak vests and carrying 12-gauge riot guns quickly stormed in through a side entrance. "You better tell 'em you're Code-Four before they start blasting away," Lyons warned her.

Officer Klein glanced over her shoulder and flipped a thumbs-up to the nearest policeman as she started to assist Lyons back onto his feet.

"Status?" a slack-jawed cop asked, halting a dozen feet away, eyes expertly scanning the restaurant.

"I'm okay," Klein said.

All the shotgun barrels dropped. Someone slipped a portable radio from its Sam Browne keeper and radioed the communications center. "Code-Four at the Chrysanthemum."

A sergeant was down on one knee between two corpses. "Cancel the paramedics," he told the officer with the portable radio. "Have Dispatch send the coroner's meat wagon instead."

"Ten-four, Sarge," the patrolman answered, smacking his bubble gum loudly as his eyes took in Klein's slender figure. "But what about her?"

As if for the first time, the field supervisor seemed to notice the bloody gash over Officer Klein's left eyebrow. "Can you drive yourself over to the ER. for some stitches or whatever it takes, Haley?" he asked her with a preoccupied frown as he began kicking warm pistols away from the dead gang members.

"I've got to process this guy," Klein said, shrugging as she indicated Carl Lyons. "I'll be okay. The bleeding's already stopped. Just a flesh wound."

Grateful that he wouldn't have to break out the black badge bands today, the sergeant glanced out through the shattered plate-glass windows. "Better keep the ambulances rolling," he said, focusing on the overturned school bus, burning butane truck and smoldering storefronts. He locked eyes with Klein. "What the hell happened out *there*?" he demanded to know, as if noticing all the commotion outside for the first time.

"The ricochets must have made it out to the street," Klein said.

"Yeah, no shit." The sergeant was tall and stocky and began shaking his head back and forth like an angry bull preparing to charge. "The paperwork on this is going to keep me at headquarters until next *month*, I'll have you know."

"Sorry, Sarge," Klein said, sounding genuinely upset, almost repentant.

The big sergeant paused in the doorway. "Aw, don't pay me no mind, Haley. The important thing is that you're okay. You *are* okay, aren't you?"

"I'll survive." She wiped beads of sweat from her blood-caked brow.

"Who's your prisoner?"

"That's the big unknown of the day. But I aim to find out," she said, forcing a smile.

"Well, speaking of your 'aim,' this looks like one righteous gundown, Deadeye. Some of the best shooting I've ever seen—for a woman." Several of the officers clustered around the corpses offered affirmative chuckles. "You done good, girl."

"It wasn't me," Klein answered, lowering her head in undeserved shame as she held out Ironman's confiscated Colt Python.

"What?"

"This guy must be Wyatt Earp incarnate or something," she said, staring at the floor. "He smoked all four of them before my .38 even cleared leather."

The sergeant paused in the doorway. "You'd better not be a cop!" he said, pointing a rigid forefinger at Lyons. When the Ironman responded with no more than a tight grin, the sergeant said, "Well, the mystery is killing me. Just who the hell *are* you, or better yet, which agency you *with*?"

Lyons lowered his eyes, too, knowing full well that mentioning Able Team right now would probably get him a straitjacket.

"Fine," the sergeant said, taking a deep breath. His eyes darted to one of the patrolmen. "Get out to my unit," he directed. "In the trunk. I want this smartass wearing ankle shackles, too."

5

Both the school bus and delivery truck drivers died in the fiery crash in front of Chinatown's Chrysanthemum Café, but miraculously none of the children received injuries serious enough to require hospitalization. Three souvenir shops across the street from the café burned to the ground before fire fighters were able to bring the ensuing blaze under control.

The street was still cordoned off when Lyons and Officer Klein returned three hours later. Ironman was minus the iron bracelets.

"Once again I'm sorry about the misunderstanding," she said as they both glanced at the Closed sign hanging in what remained of the Chrysanthemum Café's front plate-glass window.

"Forget it," Lyons said as he held the door open to a smaller, cozier restaurant. "It wasn't as if I had a badge in my wallet to get me out of the jam. You only did what I would have done under similar circumstances."

"Well, that's unlikely, and we both know it," she said, chuckling softly, "but I appreciate the thought." Heads turned as they entered. Eyes focused on Klein's uniform and the bandage over her left eye. The eyes shifted to gauge Lyons's expression as he led the way to a back table in the darkened, more romantic section of the Chinese café.

Following transportation to police headquarters three hours earlier, Lyons had requested his mandatory phone call.

"Nothing long-distance," Klein had warned.

Stony Man Farm had come to mind, but his intent hadn't been to try making contact with Brognola. Lyons's phone call was answered on the first ring. Klein didn't log the call or watch him dial, otherwise she would have noticed that it rang through to an office within the very building where they were standing.

"Robbery-Homicide," a woman's irritated voice grated, increasing the severity of his headache.

"Detective Crowe, please."

"Who's calling?" the female voice demanded.

Lyons knew he was talking to one of Crowe's fellow investigators. "Just tell him Ironman."

A note of amusement softened her tone. "Sure, Ironman, whatever you say. Hold on, honey-buns."

Lyons's eyeballs rolled toward the ceiling. It was obvious she thought he was a crank or a kook. Or worse, some back-alley snitch on crack or angel dust. It was clear Crowe kept his mouth shut about Able Team: Lyons's nickname meant nothing to her.

"Crowe here," a husky male voice crackled. "And I'm busy."

"Did the precinct princess give you my name?"

There was a slight pause on the other end of the line. "Is that you, Carl?"

"Yeah. Thanks for taking my call. I need a favor."

"Name it. Where you at?"

"The same building you're at, chump."

"Don't tell me..." A soft snicker rasped over the line.

"Booking."

"Hope you didn't murder anyone important."

"Just four first-class hoodlums, bud."

"Any local politicians? I've got a box of stale Twinkies around here somewhere. You can claim you stuffed 'em down prior to apprehension. It gets the drunk drivers off now and then."

Lyons forced the mandatory chuckle. "Naw, city hall's safe. Some gang-bangers. Down in Chinatown. Do you know Officer H.-as-in-Humdinger Klein?"

"Yeah, I'm familiar with her. Two years on the force, I think. No big busts, but she's turned in some damn good burglary supplementals. Very precise, concise and to the point, as well as—"

"Any righteous shootings lately?" Lyons asked, glancing over at Klein, who was busy filling out his fingerprint cards, her grin growing as she listened to his every word.

"None that I'm aware of. Hey, listen, Carl, not everyone can be a gunslinger like you and me, dude." Crowe laughed again.

Feeling his stare, Haley Klein glanced up from her pile of paperwork. "Your three minutes are up, hot dog. I need that phone to make an NCIC check on your pistol. So I can see where you *stole* it from," she added with a sarcastic wink. "And it better not be some poor cop's piece, or you're in for one hell of a—"

"Someone wants to talk to you," he said, holding out the phone.

"I'm not the information officer," she answered, ignoring him as she resumed filling in blanks. "Tell him to dial the complaints desk for bail-bond information, or—"

"It's Detective Crowe."

"*Chief* of Detectives Crowe?" she whispered, instantly standing.

"Right-O. He's a pal. Wants to have a few words with you."

Crowe didn't explain about Able Team, or the need to have mean men like Carl Lyons walking freely about the urban battlefields of America, armed to the teeth. Instead, he simply stated that Lyons was a government agent, was not to be detained further and that she should "most expeditiously thank her guardian angels that he was where he was *when* he was."

Klein insisted on phoning him back on the detective bureau extension, of course. She was going by the book, to ensure the voice on the other end of the line wasn't just a cleverly conceived prank to assist her prisoner in making good his escape with the jailer's blessings. It had been tried before.

But after all the formalities were completed, she thanked Crowe for his "assistance," returned Lyons's weapon and tore up the fingerprint cards.

"What about my speedloaders?" he asked, noticing she didn't trash the arrest report as well, but slipped it securely into her aluminum clipboard's inner pocket. For future reference? he wondered. Maybe she secretly liked him. Or at least his style.

"You can have the hollowpoints back later," she had said. He had hoped she'd say, "At my place." Instead, she'd said, "After we clear from the holding cell bay."

Now, as they sat in a rear booth against the back wall of the Lucky Dragon Restaurant on Clay Street, Haley Klein reached across the red tablecloth and patted his bruised knuckles. "Thanks for saving my rookie ass over there," she said, staring deeply into his eyes, seeking not romance but a friendship and loyalty all cops expected from their partners even more than from their wives or husbands.

"I don't think anyone can call you a rookie," he said, nodding to a slim Asian waitress who silently appeared from a side corridor carrying two porcelain teacups and a steaming kettle. "Two years on the street is long enough to consider you a blue line vet—especially in this goofy town." He noticed the look of mild surprise in her eyes. "Crowe told me."

"Oh."

"He also said you write good reports, better than some of the dicks up in Robbery-Homicide."

"He didn't say that," she said, smiling.

"He did. Scout's honor."

"You're no Scout." Her smile was wry as suspicion glazed her green eyes—eyes as green as the highest quality jade, Lyons decided.

"No, I suppose I'm not," he said as he inspected the menu.

"And I guess I'm supposed to be professional to the point that I don't ask any probing questions regarding your background and job description."

"Something like that."

They ordered white rice with steamed shrimp and boiled sugarcane cubes and spent more than an hour talking shop in general and, more specifically, about the shoot-out. Finally the conversation turned to a very recent case the missing persons investigators didn't seem to have time for, but which Officer Klein had taken a special interest in, if only for the boy's sake.

"The boy?" Lyons asked, genuinely curious.

And she told him about Vincent Lu and the odd occurrence at the run-down tenement at Bush and Stockton Streets, a few blocks away. "Vinnie is the little brother I never had," Haley explained. "He just loves comic books."

"What red-blooded ABC kid doesn't?"

"And I drop a batch by whenever I get some extra overtime on my paycheck." Her smile faded. "ABC?"

"American-born Chinese."

Klein's expression told him, in no uncertain terms, that she wasn't amused.

"Hey," Lyons said, laughing, "it's *their* abbreviation, not mine."

"Well," she said, her frown deepening, "Vincent was born in Vietnam, not the U.S."

"Sorry. Do I detect a soft heart beneath all that hard body armor, Officer Klein?"

She laughed softly, unexpectedly. "I told you to call me Haley."

"You got it."

"Besides," she said, dismissing his skepticism with a casual wave. "He's my Clay Street snitch, and believe me, around here a white female cop doesn't have many contacts in the...local community."

"You've got a ten-year-old informant?" Disapproval creased Lyons's features this time.

"Poor choice of words, I suppose." Her eyes dropped to the tabletop as a steaming cube of sugarcane slipped from her chopsticks.

"Here, use these," he said, sliding a box of toothpicks toward her. "No one uses chopsticks to eat sugarcane cubes. Not even ABCs."

Her smile seemed to grow slightly at his attempts to cheer her up. "Anyway, he's not really a snitch. I don't actually have him out infiltrating anyone, or naming the neighborhood dope dealer. Nothing like that. But the kid's got a good memory. And he tells me what he sees."

"And I'll bet he sees a lot."

"Everything that goes down in his part of Chinatown," she said, nodding. "Just about."

"And he saw this One-eyed Ngoc character get kidnapped?"

"From what he told me, there was definitely some sort of foul play involved. I just can't understand why Crowe's people don't seem to give a damn."

"Maybe there are more pressing cases pending in Chinatown right now," he offered.

"There are always more pressing cases pending in Chinatown," Klein said, sounding as if she were reciting a line the chief of detectives was fond of using.

"Sounds like this One-eyed Ngoc is turning into something of an obsession."

She glowered at him.

"Hey, don't get riled," he told her, instantly upset with himself.

"You might be an ex-cop, but you're still just as cynical and hard-core as all those self-styled studs I work the day watch with."

"To prove you're wrong, let's go over to Old Man Ngoc's pad and have a look-see."

"Why?" she asked, cocking a wary eye at him suspiciously. A bolt of pain from the wounded brow caused her to wince.

"You okay?" Lyons leaned forward across the table slightly and reached toward her, but Klein had leaned back in her chair, eyes tightly closed.

"Yeah, no sweat. I'll be fine. Got any aspirin?"

Lyons was already digging into his pockets. "Here, try two of these turquoise suckers."

Klein hesitated when she saw her former arrestee produce a cloudy vial with strange Oriental script on it. "What are *those*?"

"I assure you they're not on the controlled substances list, my dear."

"And that wasn't my question, *dear*."

"They're from one of the Viet herbal shops over on New Saigon Way. Clears up headaches within the hour— guaranteed. Though I've got to admit I've never used them to kill pain caused by a gunshot wound."

"I wouldn't really consider this a gunshot wound," Klein said, tapping her brow gently. "I mean—"

"Sure it is," Lyons responded quickly. "Don't be so modest. I'm going to recommend that you get a medal for what you did today, in fact."

Klein's frown returned. "Or *failed* to do, you mean. I'll be lucky if I don't get a letter of reprimand in my personnel file. I didn't even get off a shot today, remember?"

"So? Where does it say in the PD rules and regs that—"

"My sergeant is of the *old* school. Someone pulls a knife on you, you smoke him. Someone draws a gun on you, you empty all six rounds into the bastard, reload and cap off another half dozen just for good measure."

"You should switch to an automatic," he said, winking. "You could get up to twenty or more rounds at your disposal. Wouldn't have to reload."

"Not funny," she said, remaining straight-faced. "And don't change the subject. Six bullets, or twenty—I didn't drop the hammer even *once* today. *That's* what the good ol' boys on day shift will remember."

"Well, look at it this way, letters of reprimand aren't so bad."

"Oh?" she said, coating the word with unmasked skepticism.

"Listen, when I was a kick-ass cop, I'd get 'em all the time: faking radio problems whenever my sergeant tried to call off a high-speed chase and I was the lead car. Or the time Dispatch was doing car checks on graveyard shift, and my partner and I pulled over at the nearest gas station and held our portable radio next to a flushing toilet right when our unit number came up."

"You didn't." Klein appeared slightly aghast.

"Yep," Lyons said, beaming proudly. "My partner would flush and, the transmit lever still depressed, say, 'Ahhhh, *now* I'm ten-four.'"

"Oh, brother!"

"Yeah, but look, the point I'm trying to get across is that there's a Medal of Valor ribbon hanging on my den wall at home, and two fancy Certificates of Commendation, and about three dozen *framed* letters of reprimand—of which I'm the most proud, believe it or not."

"You *framed* them?" Klein giggled.

"That's a big ten-four, darlin'. My sergeant loved to give 'em out for the slightest infraction. But he was also known to proclaim that his men weren't doing their jobs unless they got at least two citizens' complaints a night."

"You've got some footlocker full of war stories, old soldier, haven't you?" Elbows on the table now, she interlocked her slender fingers and rested her chin between the two sets of feminine knuckles.

"Well, let's just pretend I'm willing to offer you access to my many years of experience."

"You were with the LAPD, right?"

He knew she hadn't forgotten. "More years than I care to remember," he said, though most of his days and nights in Los Angeles had been precious to him. At the time. Before Able Team. Now he realized there was more to life and the world and man's alleged inhumanity to man than simply the so-called City of Angels. "What about those four guys we iced this afternoon? Any idea which gang they're with? They seemed a little too old to simply be free-lance apprentices."

"None of them carried ID, of course, so we'll have to wait for the fingerprint scan to get back from the FBI, but—"

"You recognized them," he said, anticipating what she was about to say next.

"No," she said, batting her eyelashes. "But I *did* recognize a tattoo one of the coroner's people brought to my attention—behind the right ear."

"Let me guess. A dragon or a tiger. Maybe a stalk of bamboo."

"Negative. Would you believe a hissing king cobra, throat hood flared in all its glory?"

"Who uses a king cobra as their emblem?" Lyons asked.

"The Phi-Chau Gang."

"Phi-Chau?"

"It's Vietnamese for cobra. We don't see them much in Chinatown, but they wander across the invisible turf borders now and then."

"Think they're moving in on the local gangs' territory?"

"It would appear so."

"Then I'd say you're in for a lot of trouble somewhere down the line—perhaps even an all-out street war."

"That's quite possible." Klein didn't seem very concerned, however.

"Think there'll be retribution?"

"For today's massacre of four low-life snakes in the Chrysanthemum?"

"If you want to put it that way, yes."

"Perhaps. But you iced them, not me. Phi-Chau's hooters can come looking for *you*, pal, not little ol' Haley Klein."

"That's a comforting thought."

"Just kidding."

"Their friends are bound to pay the Chrysanthemum Café a visit, ask questions. Do the owners know you by name? I mean, will they ID you as the cop who interrupted the extortion shakedown?"

"I don't think the owners would say anything, but that waitress might."

Lyons grinned. "The cute, sneering one?"

"You noticed?"

"How could I miss it?"

"I don't know what she's got against me. She's always the one who brings me my tea."

"Maybe she enjoys spitting in it, back in the kitchen."

"I've wondered about that. I mean, I know a lot of these Chinese girls don't like American women—especially white women. Something about them fearing their men are attracted to us."

"I doubt if it's that at all," Lyons said, wiping his lips with a napkin. "I've never known any woman from the Far

East who felt threatened by a Western woman's beauty. Maybe you arrested her boyfriend or something.''

"I hope that's all it is."

"That's all?"

"Well, regardless...she's seen my name tag enough times. I just hope the chief keeps a news media blackout on thi afternoon's whole incident and doesn't release my name t the press."

"Once your report's filed, it becomes public record sweetie."

"Not if Crowe requests that the courts order a restrictio order on access to it—authorized law-enforcement agencie only. That kind of crap."

"I hope you're right."

"Know any good gun shops?" she asked, her eyes drift ing to the windows, and to a group of mean-looking teen agers—all clad in various shades of black—sauntering dow the sidewalk.

"What?" Lyons watched them pause to harass a schoo girl sitting on a bus bench, then jog off down a side street a a San Francisco black-and-white rounded a nearby corne on routine patrol.

"I think it's time to switch from a revolver to an auto matic."

Lyons laughed. "I see."

"Any recommendations?"

"Well, I've always been partial to Colt .45s myself. Whe my Python's not appropriate for the job, that is."

"Too much kick."

"Not at all," Lyons disagreed. "It may look like to much kick, if you're watching from the side. But whe you're actually shooting the baby yourself, well, you jus take in a deep breath and squeeze that trigger, slow an gentle, until the weapon fires itself. The resulting discharg and kick is actually quite gratifying. Gives one intense jo satisfaction, if you catch my drift."

"I think I do."

"And there's nothing to compare with the stopping power of a .45 slug, unless of course you want to be Ms. Dirty Harriet and go out and buy a .44 Magnum. Now *that* kicks."

"Well, come payday you and I got a date."

"To go shopping for a semiautomatic?"

"And target shooting afterward."

"You pack the picnic lunch?"

"Chauvinist."

"Always."

"Okay, then it's a date. But no picnic lunch. I'll bring a big can of beef jerky, and a bagful of green grapes to wash it down. No booze on the pistol range."

"I wouldn't think of it."

"You got any C-rations collecting rust at home?" she asked, her eyes narrowing.

"C-rations?"

"I know all you clandestine military types keep a store of C-rations for a rainy day, Carl. Or for your crossborder forays, right?"

"You're something else," he said, laughing warmly, happy to be with her. "Still want to traipse on over to Old Man Ngoc's pad and have a look-see?"

"You're on. Let's beat feet," she said, nodding eagerly.

6

On the way to Ngoc's apartment Haley Klein went on to explain that she had been the first uniformed officer to arrive at the scene, and that she remained puzzled by the detectives' apparent disinterest in the case. "They're dragging their feet on this one," she insisted. "They've got a blood trail, a witness—albeit he's a juvenile—and a whole apartment of physical evidence! What more could they want?"

Lyons wanted to tell her about Able Team's secret involvement in the case, and the hush-hush White House angle, but knew he couldn't. He wanted to explain that Brognola—on direct orders of the President—had dispatched him to San Francisco, that he'd been watching Ngoc's apartment building from the window of the Chrysanthemum Café when his stakeout had been interrupted by the extortion. He wanted to tell her that Crowe was one of the finest detectives on the West Coast, and that the veteran investigator had wanted to jump into this one with both boots, but was ordered to hand over the reins to Ironman.

Lyons wanted to tell her all those things, but he couldn't.

Frown deepening, he followed her up the seven flights of stairs to Ngoc's flat. Young Vincent Lu, the shoeshine boy, had been curiously absent on the ground floor when they first entered the building.

"Here, put these on, if you don't mind." She handed him a set of disposable plastic gloves before peeling back the official tape that sealed the door.

"You mean to tell me your crime lab boys haven't already dusted this joint?" Lyons asked incredulously.

"Oh, they have…they have," Klein said, nodding. "But not to *my* satisfaction—for what little *that's* worth. 'A cursory inspection of the premises,' Crowe called it. 'With no earthshaking revelations.' But once I've cracked this crazy case—"

"If there's anything to crack," Lyons cut in, feeling warmed by her smile and enthusiasm and dedication to duty. Women like Haley Klein made the best friends. He wanted to be counted as one, too.

"Yes," she said, glancing back with a bemused smirk. "*If* there's anything to crack, they'll all come running back down here, fighting over the honor to be first to apologize. Yeah, they'll definitely come running…."

"Don't hold your breath," Lyons scoffed. "Even if and when they're proven wrong, veteran cops have a nasty habit of refusing to openly acknowledge it."

"They just go on to the next unsolved case," Haley said, anticipating his follow-up remark.

"Ten-four, darlin'."

"You call me darling or sweetie one more time, Carl, and I'll be forced to respond with a choke hold." She elbowed him playfully, but her tone had been no-nonsense.

"So sorry, ma'am."

"You're probably right, though. But I can fantasize, can't I?"

The innocent innuendo shrouding her words caused them both to blush, and Ironman quickly changed the subject. "That the blood trail there?"

"What's left of it."

But he wasn't really listening to her words now. As she dropped to one knee beside the jagged crimson stain, Carl found himself staring at the outline of her fine curves, inspecting her flawless profile—flawless even for a law enforcer. No one had broken her nose yet. He hoped no one ever did. She was in her mid-thirties—Crowe had revealed as much—but she could still pass for a much younger college girl, fresh out of high school, and he wondered why she had chosen policework as a career at this point in her life. Perhaps she was a lateral transfer, he decided. Maybe she'd spent five or ten years with the Oakland or San Jose PD, prior to joining the San Francisco force. "Guess it doesn't really matter," he muttered under his breath.

"Pardon?" she asked, glancing back up at him.

"Nothing," he said, unlocking the sliding glass doors and stepping out onto the balcony. "So tell me, where do you hope to take this case from here?"

She joined him on the balcony and reached out, testing the fire escape. It jiggled a bit, but otherwise seemed firmly attached to the side of the building. "Well, officially I'm not on the case at all. I'd probably get canned if my watch commander knew I was even here—and rightly so. But I just feel there's more to this thing than a missing persons case. And now Vinnie's gone, too."

"Kids vanish. We can check back again tonight. Later."

"We?" Her eyes locked onto his and, in the distance, a siren began its mournful wail.

"Well...I'm taking some vacation time this week, and with nothing better to do..."

Klein's bright green eyes narrowed. "And just what, kind sir, *were* you doing at the Chrysanthemum Café this afternoon? I suppose you just happened to be there by chance."

"You could say that," Lyons answered as he glanced out at the setting sun.

"Sure, you just happened to be in the right place at the right time to smoke four low-life Oriental goons." Her words were soaked with sarcasm.

"Something like that." He draped a hand casually on her shoulder and motioned out to sea. "You know, down in the tropics the natives tell their children that, at sunset, if they listen carefully, they'll be able to hear the ocean start to boil when the sun sinks into the horizon.''

"And who told *you* that? Some tanned and topless island maiden with nothing more than a fern covering her privates?''

"My mama.''

"Sure.''

Carl smiled. "Trust me. But keep your eyes open.''

"No need for trust,'' she said as she turned away and walked back into the apartment just as the sunset was turning its most romantic shade of molten gold. Lyons wondered about her last love, and how bad it had hurt her. What man in his right mind would leave a beautiful woman like Haley Klein in the first place?

"So what's our next move?'' he asked, following her in off the balcony and quietly closing the sliding glass doors. But he was unable to take his eyes off the great orange orb throwing red and pink pastels across the western sky as it disappeared from view. The Pacific's murky blue line marked the edge of Ironman's world for now.

"Why were you at the café?'' Unsmiling, she turned to face him. "Were you staking it out for extortionists? Is that it? You're with the Metro Asian Gang Task Force or something, right?''

"You know I can't reveal to you what or why or—''

"Sure you can. We're both cops, Carl. Level with me. It's not as if some colossal national security secret was involved or something!''

He hoped his expression hadn't changed. "I'm not a cop.''

"You're close enough. You're more cop than any man on my shift. And if you're not a cop, you should be.''

"Haley…'' He lifted a hand, palm out, sensing the inevitable outburst that was to come, hoping to silence her.

"Damn it, Carl! You saved my life down there today!" She moved toward him, not unlike a panther pouncing, but she melted the moment she was in his arms.

He glanced around the unfamiliar living room as he felt her letting go now, finally, after all these hours. But there was no couch or chair to gently let her down onto, so he just held her as the sobs racked her body and the tears cascaded down her cheeks.

"Let it out," he said, stroking her hair, knowing how it felt, knowing the heart-thumping joy of escaping the grave, cheating Lady Death by inches, moments. He knew how the shock of it all finally struck only hours later after the adrenaline high had worn off and you finally came back down to earth, a different person, forever changed by a moment of gunplay, an instant of glory.

She wasn't attracted to him. Not yet. For now he was her father, brother, son, protector—the man who'd snatched her from the jaws of death—and, in his arms, everything became all right again. Everything became sane once more.

"I'm sorry." Her hands came up between their bodies, her palms pressing against his chest now, pushing the two of them apart. "I didn't mean to..." But he held her close, tightly, ignoring the trembling in her arms and breasts as she pressed them nearly flat against his chest once more.

"It's okay," he said, staring out through the sliding glass doors, watching the sun leave them as it continued on across the Pacific, no doubt sending its first shafts of dawn down across the misty Orient at that very moment.

"You've been through this many times before, haven't you?" she asked, her voice cracking as the tears welled up in her eyes again. "This shoot-out stuff's old hat to you, isn't it?"

"I wouldn't exactly say that."

"Don't tell anybody about what just happened, okay?" She drew her head back and stared up into his eyes. "About me breaking down...cracking up like this. Please?"

"What just happened is perfectly natural, Haley. It's called stress fatigue. You've just survived a pretty traumatic incident, you know."

"Don't psychoanalyze me, okay?"

"I was just—"

"Make love to me, Carl."

He felt a chill run up and down his spine. His involuntary swallow was dry, and loud enough for her to hear, but she didn't laugh or even smile. There was desperation on her face, fear in her eyes. "Here?" he asked, feeling a warm sensation swirl through his loins. "At a crime scene?"

"You don't want me?" she asked quietly. "You don't . . . *desire* me?"

"I think there's some kind of law against doing it at a crime scene still sealed with evidence tape." He sought technicalities, bogus legal excuses, anything, even though he knew Haley would see right through him.

"It's the uniform, isn't it?" she said, hastily unbuttoning her unflattering topcoat.

"No, no, it's..." He grabbed one of her wrists before she even had a couple of buttons undone. "I'd be taking advantage of you," he said, guiding her back toward the balcony and cool, fresh air, hoping it would act like a slap against the face. "Haley, did your parents name you after the comet?"

"After the British actress," she said, sounding mesmerized, far off, as she stared through him. "You know," she said, her voice wavering, "Hayley Mills, the bubbly little blond girl in all those Walt Disney mysteries. Of course, my name's spelled differently."

"Yes, of course," he said, nodding compassionately. "It fits."

"She was my father's favorite movie star. Mother wanted to name me Loretta. Loretta Young was *her* favorite."

"Parents can be so silly sometimes."

"Yes."

As Haley turned to look out at the deepening purple of twilight, she let out a sudden laugh. To Carl it sounded like a bittersweet cry for help. "This is crazy," she said. "I can't *believe* what I just did . . . what I just said."

"You didn't do . . . didn't say anything." He gently took hold of her chin and brought her gaze back up into his eyes. "It was all in your imagination. Nothing happened. Absolutely nothing."

She sighed, feigning great relief. "Oh, I'm so glad to hear you say *that*, Carl Lyons."

"I'm going to count to three and when I snap my fingers you'll return from never-never land. Got it?"

"Yes," she said, playing along, rising on her toes. "Do I click my heels together, too?"

"If you so desire."

"Then I'm ready." Her face seemed to glow, despite the trickle of blood now working its way down from the bandage covering her brow, and Lyons knew he was staring at one of the street war's walking wounded.

"One . . ."

"Thank you, Carl," she sighed, closing her eyes tightly.

"Two . . ."

"Thank you for being here when I needed someone. There's no one else, you know. No one."

"Three . . ." He paused, forgetting to snap his fingers as he reflected on what she had just said.

Head hanging back, Haley just stood there in anticipation until he closed his own eyes and kissed her.

"That was nice," she said a moment later. "Now I'll bet you're married with eight kids, right?"

Lyons laughed openly, breaking the embrace. "Hardly," he said, lifting his left hand.

"No tan line around the ring finger," she said, nodding. "Which these days means absolutely nothing."

"Perhaps," he said, frowning. "And then again it could mean anything you want it to."

"Yes..." Haley turned away and moved slowly toward One-eyed Ngoc's bedroom. "Come in here," she said a few seconds later after he had busied himself examining a stack of the missing tenant's unopened mail sitting on the television. "I want to show you something."

Grinning, Lyons envisioned her lying back on the bed—if indeed there even was one—her uniform already hanging over the headboard. Snap out of it, Ironman, he chastised himself. She's probably got a perfectly good reason for calling you into the bedroom.

Klein was standing next to the dresser, fully clothed, when he entered. "Check this out," she said, handing him an address book. "There are only three names in it—two with addresses, one with just a phone number."

Lyons accepted the tiny black book, smaller than the palm of his hand, and moved toward the telephone. "The notation above the phone number's in Chinese," he said.

"Don't look at me," she said, shrugging. "I can barely get by with proper English grammar these days."

Frowning at her response, he picked up the phone and was relieved to hear a dial tone. One-eyed Ngoc paid his bills. The number had a 212 area code—Manhattan. He completed the long-distance call and waited, listening to eight, nine, ten unanswered rings.

"The Vietnamese Association," an older woman's voice finally answered.

Lyons replaced the receiver, breaking the connection.

"Anybody answer?" Klein asked.

"No," he replied smoothly, his tone offering no reason for her to doubt him. "Busy signal. I'll try again later."

"What about the two addresses?"

"One's on Bolsa Avenue, down in Garden Grove."

"Orange County, south of L.A.?"

"Right."

"Why does that ring a bell?" she asked.

"The Bolsa Strip's the main artery running through the heart of Little Saigon."

"Vietnamese refugees, you mean?"

"Yes. Bolsa runs east and west through the suburbs of Santa Ana, Garden Grove and Westminster. About a hundred thousand refugees have made the area their home. Largest resettlement of ethnic, full-blooded Viets in the country, actually."

"Full-blooded? You mean to tell me there's a difference?"

"Just east of L.A., in the San Gabriel Valley, another sixty-five thousand Viets of Chinese extraction have resettled in the connecting communities of Monterey Park, Alhambra, Rosemead and Temple City." He glanced at the address in the phone book again. "The hundred block's about right."

"You've got every ethnic enclave in Southern California pegged down to the exact hundred block?" she said, feigning surprise. "I'm impressed."

"We had a case down there a few months back. We were back and forth like Ping-Pong balls between the Vietnamese hangouts and Vandenberg and . . . I mean . . ."

"We?" She was smiling ear to ear now.

"Well, the hundred block checks out, anyway. There's no name with the address, just *dai khai*, which is Vietnamese for *general*. General, as in one star, I presume. Probably something to do with the freedom fighters down there. The Resistance or something."

But Haley Klein wasn't listening to any of his verbal tactics of distraction. "Vandenberg?" she wondered out loud. "*You* were part of that antiterrorist team that kept the space shuttle *Atlantis* from being blown to bits by the KGB's Skylink device, right? The commandos every newspaper in America wrote front-page stories about for a week without ever really being able to find out a single thing about who they were, where they came from or what any of them looked like?"

"This third name here," he said, staring down at the phone book, expression noncommittal, "is Tran Van Thieu, with a nearby address. I think we should check it out. No phone's listed."

"You're going to keep changing the subject," she surmised. "You're going to keep me in the dark about your background, about your boss and your current mission and all that secret agent shit, right?"

He glanced up at her and smiled grimly. "Something like that."

"So, as far as I'm supposed to be concerned, you're just along for the ride." She folded both arms over her breasts and tilted her head slightly to one side. "And *I'm* still in charge."

"Let me put it this way, Haley," Lyons said, patting the Python holstered under his jacket. "If the shit gets too deep, I'll let Mr. Colt out of his corral again."

It took them ten minutes to walk down through the heart of Chinatown to the address found in One-eyed Ngoc's little black book. Again it was an apartment house. Tran Van Thieu resided on the top floor. Like Ngoc's apartment, it was on the seventh level.

"Must be for good luck," Lyons surmised.

"But the Chinese consider eight the luckiest number," Klein advised him. "Don't they?"

"This may be Chinatown, Haley, but Ngoc and Tran are Vietnamese names," he reminded her.

The door to room 722 was locked, but there was no dead bolt, and Lyons quickly produced a pick.

"Shouldn't we at least notify the apartment manager that we plan to enter the place?" Klein asked him. "I mean, we don't really have much probable cause to go around—"

She went silent when Lyons dropped to one knee and began sniffing along the cracks in the door.

"What is it?"

"Corpse," he replied simply.

"Corpse?" Klein's hand went to her gun holster.

"I've been on enough dead body calls to know when there's a ripe corpse waiting for me inside a house or apartment. I'm surprised none of the neighbors have phoned it in. Maybe the odor's not bad enough yet for them to get involved."

"But I still think—"

"Go ahead and notify the apartment manager downstairs of my suspicions," Lyons said, sighing. "Meantime..." He began working on the doorknob lock.

By the time Officer Klein returned with the manager—an old, stooped Puerto Rican woman with curlers in her hair and a barking Chihuahua under one arm—Lyons was standing inside.

The apartment manager screamed when she saw the headless corpse of a nude female lying on its back in front of an expensive bookcase.

7

The apartment was empty except for the decapitated corpse and a few items of Spartan furniture, which had been up-ended and tossed about. Cushions had been cut open, paneling stripped away, drawers emptied. In short, the apartment had been ransacked.

Without a head, determining exact age would have to wait for an autopsy, but based on his cursory examination of the body's overall physical condition in general and the hands in particular, Lyons estimated the age category at time of death to be somewhere in the range of twenty-five to thirty-five.

"What kind of monster could hack her head off like that?" Haley Klein asked, her heart still racing.

"It wasn't *hacked*," Lyons, who was down on one knee examining the wound, answered. "It was *sliced*, neatly and efficiently, probably with a surgeon's scalpel or..." His voice trailed off.

"I meant, who could remove a woman's head in the first place? I mean...you know exactly what I mean."

"Make that a sword. Not a scalpel. A sword. Maybe a broadsword, although that would probably be too large to drag in and out of the building without attracting attention. But definitely something sharp and heavy. It would take something *very* sharp and *very* heavy to make this clean a cut."

Klein dropped to one knee beside him. "How so?"

"Have you ever had the opportunity to lop off some-one's head?" he asked, locking eyes with her.

"Not recently," she returned, glancing away as an icy shiver went through her.

"It's not an easy task. You can't just walk up to some-one, for instance, and stab him in the throat with a butcher knife and hope to see the head roll away. There's a lot of bone and gristle and meat and muscle holding the skull to the neck, not to mention all the veins and arteries and fat globules and—"

"I think I get the message." She wasn't sure if he was trying to be funny or not.

"What I'm trying to say is that only an expert could de-liver a single blow the way this woman was struck, and so neatly sever the cranium. Someone with an executioner's mentality." He was thinking of some hooded henchman standing beside a chopping block in a mist-shrouded dun-geon gallows during the Dark Ages.

"A professional," Klein said. "A medical doctor maybe? A surgeon?"

"Possible. But not probable. I've seen emergency room physicians at work, for instance. A surgeon—even a de-mented, psychotic doctor who'd flipped out and gone off the edge, for whatever reason, would still go about cutting his intended victim up differently. With even *more* preci-sion. We're talking seal up the loose ends, okay?" Lyons motioned toward the blood-smeared floor. "He—or she—wouldn't have allowed that pool of blood. At least that's my gut feeling. I could be wrong. I'm only human. I've been wrong before."

"That's a comforting thought." Officer Haley Klein rose and walked toward a bureau lying on its side against the far wall. Above it hung a tapestry of Vietnam: bright oils on black velvet, depicting small children playing on the back of a ponderous water buffalo as the animal, mired to the shoulders in rice paddy muck, used its long tail to swat at a cluster of multicolored dragonflies hovering over its haunches.

"You have any problem with me checking it out?" she asked, gesturing toward the bureau.

"Good idea." He stood back up to join her. "But it looks like somebody already cleaned this entire place out. I doubt there's anything of value left—materialistically speaking *or* of an intelligence nature—and..."

"What about..." the apartment manager stammered. "I mean, the body there. What about the body? You can't just leave it there!"

"She's not going anywhere," Lyons said, not bothering to glance over at the doorway as he helped Klein right the bureau.

"Thank you for your assistance, ma'am," the police-woman said, staring at the wide-eyed woman standing in the doorway. "You can go now. We'll handle this from here on in."

"And, ma'am," Lyons said, turning to face her. "I'd appreciate it if you wouldn't discuss what you saw here with the other tenants. Not right now, anyway, okay?"

Eyeballs rolling skyward, the woman crossed herself and, muttering in rapid Spanish, stalked off down the hallway. At the stairwell she paused when stopped by an apartment dweller down the hallway, and they began jabbering non-stop. Lyons recognized the words *dead woman* and *no head* in Spanish. He could only shake his own.

"And what have we here?" Lyons said as he detected the faint sound of something hitting the floor beneath the bureau just as it was being righted. "Turn this sucker back over onto its side."

"But it's heav—"

"Just do it, girl."

They hadn't even tipped the dresser back a few inches before the small pocket diary came into view. After the bureau was lying on its side again, Lyons examined a slot in the bottom layer of wood supporting the base. It was the same shade of dark brown as the diary's cover. "Whoever ransacked this place missed what they were looking for."

"But we didn't," Klein said, sounding nervous that such unexpected luck on their part could only be a bad omen of things to come. This was, after all, Chinatown.

Using only his fingertips, Lyons carefully lifted the diary and held it against the three-by-four-inch slot. "Perfect fit," he said. Then, just as cautiously—so as not to disturb any fingerprints that might be on the covers, as well as leave his own—Ironman gently began paging through the small journal.

"Thank God it's in English," Klein noted as he skipped from the preceding year's entries to the current month.

"Writing, conversing in English instead of Vietnamese or Chinese can be somewhat of a status symbol of sorts for new immigrants," he explained. "I visited an ESL class once."

"ESL?"

"English as a Second Language. They're taught at a lot of the refugee centers. Anyway, the students are sometimes encouraged to keep a diary in English. Nothing special. Just a couple of paragraphs each night before they retire—just to make sure they put what they learn into practice."

"And you think the owner of this diary was an ESL student?"

"Quite possibly." Lyons searched for a name in the book, but there was none. "Does this look like the handwriting of a man or a woman to you?"

"Definitely male. Look at the block letters. If I didn't know better, I'd say he was a cop. They teach cops to write like that, you know."

"They *re*teach them," Lyons said, chuckling. "Yeah, don't I know it. Well, maybe whoever authored this baby *is* a cop."

"Let's hope not."

"'Mau is compromised. General Pham is compromised,'" Lyons read from a week-old entry in the diary. "'Everyone is compromised....'"

"Mau," Klein said, nodding. "That would be Ngoc Ung Mau—the missing guy. One-eyed Ngoc, the kid calls him."

"'The whole operation is compromised. I sense a noose tightening, a net closing in on Mot Bo Bay, and I've no way of knowing if the enemy has become our own people or the same old nemesis with a new mask. Mau has been instructed that if he does not hear from me the List of Fourteen should be moved to a safe place—per orders from the General.'"

"Mot Bo Bay?" Klein focused on the words. "Another name?"

"Sounds like an outfit to me," Lyons said, shaking his head. "An organization, but that's just based on the way he's penned this entry."

"I wonder who he considers his 'own people,' or 'the same old nemesis.'"

Lyons stared at the monogrammed initials on the diary's cover: TVT. Pol and Gadgets should have picked up Tran Van Thieu by now, he was thinking. In New York. Lyons glanced over at the dead woman. Could Tran have sliced off her head—for whatever reason—and flown all the way to the east coast just to pass more documents? And why? Why go to all the trouble? "North Vietnamese soldiers were fond of keeping diaries," Lyons told Klein. "Even onto the battlefield they carried them. Their superiors prohibited it, of course, but they still kept them—often stuffed with photos of fellow soldiers or the girls they left behind. I'll never understand why hard-core regulars like the NVA could be so sentimental about logging the day-to-day activities of their unit, their buddies."

"You're saying you think Van Thieu is a Communist? A former North Vietnamese soldier?"

"I'm not saying anything. It was just a thought."

The sound of heavy boots and shoes rushing up a stair-well reached their ears, and soon the doorway was filled with grim-faced men in uniforms, brandishing handguns. One of the officers spotted Klein's police uniform and motioned for the other patrolmen to holster their pistols. "We got a dead body call at this address," he said, staring down at the headless corpse. His eyes shifted to Klein's, then back to the nude body. "Any truth to that rumor?"

None of the cops had entered yet. They remained crowded just outside the doorway as if to say that Klein—as first officer on the scene—could certainly have the call if she wanted it. "We're not sure just exactly *what* we have here," she said as Lyons discreetly slipped the diary into a back pants pocket. "We were working on something unrelated." Envisioning an irate Chief of Detectives Crowe berating her for meddling in affairs that didn't concern her, a cover story began formulating in her head. "At least we thought it was unrelated. We ended up here on a welfare check. Management let us in. I'm off duty."

"Heard about your shooting, Haley," the senior patrolman said as he finally entered the apartment after motioning his backups to remain in the hallway. He didn't want anyone to disturb any evidence at the scene. "How's the eyebrow?" A slight grin twisted one side of his mouth.

"I'll live," she replied with an unamused frown.

The patrolman stared down at the corpse. His nostrils wrinkled at the odor of death. "Well, we definitely don't have natural causes here, dear."

"No, we don't. I don't know just exactly *what* you've got here, *dear*. But we'll be going."

"You didn't leave any prints on anything, did you?" The grin became an ear-to-ear smile.

"Of course not," Klein said, heading for the door, and the men crowding it backed away to let the officer and Lyons through.

"Well, just be sure and write me up a supplemental on what brought you here in the first place," the district officer called after her with a laugh. "For the record. If that wouldn't be too much to ask, dearie."

"You got it, *dearie*," Klein said acidly, punctuating her assurance with a mildly obscene gesture on her way out through the door.

As she and Carl Lyons headed for the stairwell, there was a general snicker that ran through the five or six patrolmen watching her leave. Someone sent a low-key wolf whistle bouncing off the hallway walls, but neither Haley nor her newfound friend looked back.

ACROSS THE STREET from Tran Van Thieu's apartment building two well-groomed, light-skinned Asian men in expensive three-piece suits stood in the shadows of a storefront's entryway. They watched Lyons and the uniformed policewoman exit through a ground-floor security gate that someone had left wide open. Blocking the roadway in front of the building, a half-dozen locked SFPD radio cars sat idling, their roof lights flashing sluggishly.

The two Asians were in their late forties. One wore wire-rim glasses and an innocent almost boyish expression. He smiled constantly. The other sported a pencil-thin jet-black mustache, and a collection of deep scars crisscrossing his left cheek. His perpetual frown was in blatant contrast to his companion's cheerful countenance.

"Do you think they visited Tran's apartment, Comrade?" the man with glasses asked in soft-spoken but fluent English.

"Of course they did," returned the unsmiling Vietnamese, who was unable to hide his heavy accent. "They would have no other reason to rush from Ngoc's building straight to this one."

"Yes, of course. Most certainly. But do you think they found anything? Anything that might lead them to Tran, or the List of Fourteen?"

"Nonsense," the other man said. "We searched Tran's apartment from floor to ceiling. There was nothing."

"It was a pity about the woman." The scholarly-looking man's ever-present smile faded somewhat as he thought of the young woman.

"She was nothing but a whore. Servicing him. Tran has forsaken the Communist way. He has become a capitalist, delighting in the materialistic pursuits and pleasures of the flesh that capitalists always spoil themselves with. Besides, she wouldn't talk. She had plenty of opportunity to answer my questions, yet she refused to speak. Not one word. Except all those obscene profanities."

The man with the glasses chuckled, but his comrade silenced him with a quick glare. "Perhaps she was one of our own agents. I find it hard to believe a common street tramp would have been so hard to crack. No prostitute would feel so much loyalty to any man—regardless of whether or not he was providing her with food and a roof over her head."

"Don't forget the angel dust."

"Yes, the angel dust, too. But did you have to tease her with it, and *then* chop off her head? I'll never forget how you carried her head out onto the balcony and nonchalantly dropped it into a passing garbage truck seven flights below!"

Taking his comrade's comment as a compliment, the man with the scars on his left cheek smiled for the first time as he watched Able Team commando Carl Lyons and San Francisco Police Officer Haley Klein round a distant corner and vanish into the Chinatown crowds.

POL BLANCANALES AND GADGETS SCHWARZ stood with the sun to their backs and the wind in their faces as they watched the Lear jet taxi out onto Rockpoint Airfield's main east-west runway on the edge of New York City. Inside the government plane Tran Van Thieu sat between two heavily armed escorts for the short ride to Stony Man Farm, where he would undergo a further debriefing at the hands of Hal Brognola.

Tran was a tough cookie, but Brognola was tougher. The Chief knew all the latest tricks. There was only so much Tran could prepare for mentally. Now it was only a matter of time. And expertise.

8

Carl Lyons sat on a brown leather sofa, its back to the living room wall of Haley Klein's third-floor apartment on the east edge of Chinatown. From his position Lyons could glance to the left, straight down the narrow hallway to the bathroom at the end. The bathroom door was open. Haley, clad in only a towel, was stepping toward a shower, the water running. Or Lyons could glance to the right, toward the balcony that looked out onto San Francisco Bay. And in the balcony's sliding glass doors he would again see Haley's reflection—a different one now as the white towel fluttered to the floor. No tan lines marred her bronzed flesh, and he wondered if she sunbathed on the balcony here, or at some private beach along the ocean.

Lyons attempted, once more, to concentrate on the diary in his lap.

From the building where they had discovered the headless corpse, Lyons and the policewoman had proceeded on foot to her apartment half a mile away. Initially he found it odd that a tall blonde would choose to live in a building that appeared, at first glance, to be occupied predominantly by Asians. But when she explained that the department preferred its police officers to reside within the city limits—and she personally felt a *good* cop would also choose to live among the people he or she served—Lyons had to concur with her reasoning.

His eyes rose from the diary as thoughts again swirled through his head. He'd read an entire chapter without comprehending any of it, only his own thoughts...only what Haley had told him. Lyons again found himself staring first at the balcony reflection, then directly down the hallway at the open door. Beyond it, nothing separated him from the hard-bodied, finely toned woman except a shower curtain.

It was a filmy white curtain, with thin bamboo reed designs and, though staring at her now was almost like peering through frosted glass, there was no mistaking the firm curves. He wondered if she was acting this way by design—if the open bathroom door was an invitation. Or if the day's events had simply reduced her to the scatterbrained state—as Gadgets called it—and she hadn't realized her carelessness. Perhaps she was running on automatic pilot right now, as if she were alone in the apartment. Ironman dismissed her behavior. "If you want me, come and get me," he whispered under his breath with a chuckle, attention returning to the diary.

On one of the last pages Tran had drawn a crude map, showing his apartment and that of One-eyed Ngoc. Lyons recognized the intersections involved—all were here in Chinatown—but he wasn't sure about many of the references noted at specific locations. They were in Vietnamese or Chinese.

A secondary map seemed to depict something underground—a tunnel, perhaps. And there were measurements jotted down here and there, in everything from meters to inches. One rough sketch appeared to represent building blocks of one sort or another, and behind the blocks, two letters: SW. Initials? Or simply an abbreviation of some sort? Southwest? Shitty weather? Hell, it could be just about anything, he decided.

His ears detected an odd, offbeat tune, which he pinpointed as coming from the bathroom. Haley was singing in the shower. A good sign, Lyons thought. Get it out of your system, girl. Sing your cares away....

Rising, he walked over to her phone. From this corner of the living room she wouldn't be able to see him. Make sure she keeps singing, he reminded himself before picking up the receiver. Make sure the shower water is still running.

Using a predetermined set of coded numbers, Lyons dialed into a scrambled cellular network that was bounced off a military satellite and sent back down directly to Stony Man Farm.

Cowboy Kissinger answered, and he soon had Hal Brognola in the room.

"Carl!" Brognola said, sounding somewhere between relaxed and anxious. "We've been waiting for you to check in."

"Yeah, well, things have been kind of hectic here in San Francisco lately. Have we located Tran Van Thieu?"

"That's what I've been waiting to tell you," Brognola replied. "We finally grabbed him up in the Big Apple."

"New York?" Lyons concentrated on the sound of shower water and Haley's off-key humming. The off-duty policewoman had switched from "Moon River" to "She Works Hard for Her Money."

"Yeah, near the office of the Vietnamese Association. Your call brought me out of the interrogation chamber. He's putting up the usual resistance, but he's not as tough a cookie as he's trying desperately to portray. We'll try some trick questions first, then a truth-or-consequences session."

"I'd tell you to enjoy yourself, but I know you don't need my encouragement."

"Life's full of little mandatory pains. We do what we have to do, and go on from there. Anyway, like I said, I've been waiting for you to check in. Gadgets and Politician are already airborne, en route to California and your location. I'm sending them over to assist."

"Roger. Tango Yankee, Chief," he replied.

"Don't thank me. Thank Crowe. I just got off the phone with San Francisco PD's super dick. He thinks you're in for one righteous world of hurt, Carl. He says you'd better watch your ass out on the street."

"Yeah, so what else is new?"

"New? I'll tell you what's new. Some San Francisco beat cop rousted a carload of Vietnamese gang-bangers parked outside a joint called the Chrysanthemum Café only a couple of hours ago."

"So?" He thought about the group of punks he and Haley had watched harassing the schoolgirl at the bus bench earlier.

"In the trunk of their car was a shitload of AK-47 assault rifles."

"Well, I didn't expect 'em to be packing peashooters."

"And a cardboard box containing over a thousand recently copied flyers—still warm to the touch."

"Flyers?"

"Bounty posters, Ironman. Crude facsimiles of two departmental file photos."

"Let me guess," Lyons said, sounding suddenly depressed as his ears detected "Girls Just Want to Have Fun" coming from the shower in an out-of-tune crescendo.

Brognola didn't grant him the guess. "Yours and Patrolwoman Haley Klein's. Watch your back, Carl."

The deep sigh left a pain in his chest as Lyons replaced the receiver and sat back heavily on the nearest chair. Bounty posters? *That* hadn't exactly been in the cards for this mission, had it? And yet, there never seemed to be any smooth sailing for the commandos of Able Team. Never.

"I hope it wasn't long-distance."

When he glanced up with a start, Carl found Haley standing at the edge of the living room, dripping wet, wrapped in a waterlogged towel. His eyes dropped to the swells just below the towel's top edge, then rose again to gauge her expression.

"Just a l-local call," he stuttered, feeling the flush and mentally reprimanding himself at the momentary slip in confidence. "To a . . . friend. Sorry."

"You're not gay, are you?"

"Hardly, my dear," he answered, his eyes dropping to the jutting breasts again. "In fact, I'm feeling a hundred percent full of the right combination of hormones right now and—"

"Then there's nothing to be sorry about." She smiled, whirled and pranced back toward the bathroom—the clandestine phone call forgotten. "I called out for you to grab me a new bottle of shampoo from the sink," she said. "I've run out. But you didn't answer."

"Sorry. Your singing kind of had me hypnotized there for a while. Do you still want to grab something to eat?"

"I'm almost ready!" she called back tauntingly. "Cut me some slack. We're not married yet."

From her reflection in the balcony's sliding glass doors he could see that she'd donned a wraparound Malaysian-style sarong and was preparing to blow-dry her hair.

Lyons glanced at his wristwatch. "Women," he muttered under his breath as the loud contraption drowned out his words.

AT THE LUCKY DRAGON RESTAURANT Lyons told her about the bounty flyers. "Wanted posters?" she said, laughing. "On little ol' me? Hell, I've got to get hold of one of those for my scrapbook, Carl. I've just got to!"

Her reaction left Ironman somewhat taken aback.

"So what's our plan of attack after the dim sum?" he asked, nodding down at their nearly empty plates.

"I guess it's between Clint Eastwood and Charles Bronson," she replied, scanning the local cinema advertisements in the *San Francisco Chronicle*.

"You know what I mean."

The firmness in his tone made Haley lower the newspaper. Expression serious, she locked eyes with the stranger from Stony Man Farm. "I guess..."

"Yes?"

"We return to the apartment house..."

"Which one?"

"One-eyed Ngoc's," she replied.

"Why?"

"Why not?" she countered.

Lyons's face contorted with a crease of irritation. "Why not Tran's place? Why not—"

"I get the feeling that you're not telling me everything, Carl," Haley interrupted. "I want you to level with me."

"Haley..."

"Don't 'Haley' me, buster. Listen, I looked the other way when you removed that damn diary, that damn piece of evidence from the scene of a homicide, because Chief of Detectives Crowe more or less vouched for you. But now I'm getting tired of playing the dutiful, outranked civilian cop tagging along with Master Spy Maxwell Smartass. I'm beginning to feel like Secret Agent 99—and I don't like being kept in the dark. Not when my life's at stake. Not when—"

"When there's a bounty on your head?" Lyons laughed softly, and people at the other tables lost interest.

She seemed to calm down, then asked, "Well?"

"Forget it."

"Forget what?"

"I can't talk about it. Listen, Haley... were you ever in the military?"

"How'd you know?" she asked, cocking an eyebrow at him.

"I didn't. I was just asking. Okay, so what branch were you in? Army MPs, right?"

"Air Force."

"Air Cops? I mean, law-enforcement specialists or SPs or just what exactly."

"I worked for the Army's equivalent of MI."

"Military Intelligence?"

"Right."

"Perfect."

"Perfect, my ass. Where's this leading to, Carl, 'cause I'm in no mood to—"

"You were in Air Force Intelligence," he said, waving her silent, "and there were times you couldn't tell anyone what you were even doing, much less the specific case you were working on, right?"

"But—" she started to protest, her green eyes beginning to bulge like glowing emeralds.

"Just answer my question. In fact, it's not necessary. I already know the answer, and the answer is...*was* yes. You couldn't divulge which outfit you were with, or what project you were currently risking your life to protect or solve or whatever. Now I just want you to look back on those times for a second. I know they were enjoyable, rewarding times and, like most wingnuts and skycops, you yearn to return—"

"I hated my four years in the Air Force," she revealed. "Nothing but a shitload of oversexed eighteen-year-old airmen running around all the time trying to screw everything in a skirt. I felt like I was on a farm or something, like I was *running* the damn farm, and always trying to keep the bulls separated from the cows, or unlock the dogs. Do you know what I mean?"

Lyons tried not to smile. Glancing away, he said, "Yeah, I suppose I do. I guess I tend to forget that a soldier's life overseas...well, a man's life is different than a woman's and—"

"I was stationed at Lowry Air Force Base."

"Where's that? Alaska?"

"Just about. Aurora, Colorado, just east of Denver. The only time it got 'exotic' was when the Oriental hookers sneaked on base to try to pull discount tricks at the NCO Club. But, okay, so I get your drift. You're not going to tell me who you work for or why you're here and what kind of shit I'm about to blindly step into, right?"

"Something like that," Lyons said, grinning. "But I promise you one thing," he began, downing the last of his Vietnamese coffee and wiping his lips with a napkin in a rough, manly sort of way that aroused Haley, "if anything happens out there on the street, and I think there's anything you should know that would help you—or us—survive the situation, I won't hold back. On that I promise."

"Fair enough," she agreed. She stood, dug into her pockets and threw some bills on the table. "And I promise not to be so nosy in the future." Her features had softened somewhat. "It's just that it really irks me when I'm faced with a mystery and I can't break somebody's arm to get at the facts."

"Want to arm-wrestle?" he asked as he sat back down and plopped his elbow on the tabletop. "Get it out of your system?"

"You ought to be doing stand-up comedy at a club," she said, tugging him back to his feet.

Lyons removed his wallet from his back pocket.

"Forget it," Haley said. "My treat."

"But—"

"It's the least I can do," she said, winking. "For saving my unworthy ass today."

"Anyone ever tell you that sometimes you talk like a damn street cop?"

"Only other street cops. And *ex*-street cops."

"Touché!"

"Okay, here's the plan," she said as they began walking past the bar lounge toward the cashier. "We scope out One-eyed Ngoc's place. Canvass the entire apartment building.

Question everything that moves. You know how the Chinese are. Someone somewhere was bound to have seen something sometime.''

"But getting them to talk—especially to us—might not be so easy," Lyons told her.

"I know, but it's the only plan I've got right now. Are you game?''

"I'm always—"

Lyons's words were drowned out by the roar of a car passing by outside the restaurant. Irritated, he glanced at the plate-glass window to their left, just as it exploded.

A burst of bullets danced across the countertop on their right, destroying dozens of liquor bottles lined up in front of a long mirror. The entire lounge was showered with shards and slivers of glass as empty beer mugs and wine and whiskey glasses hanging from a suspended storage rack overhead exploded.

Screaming in terror and confusion, patrons seated at nearby tables scattered for cover. One woman collapsed directly in front of them. A large halo of crimson appeared on her pink chiffon dress between her shoulder blades as she dropped lifelessly against a lobster tank display inside the front foyer. Lyons watched her head bounce off the aquarium's thick glass on the way down. The aquarium spiderwebbed, but the glass held.

They both dropped into a squat, both drew their concealed weapons, both glanced around, assessing the situation in a blink of an eye, then started quickly toward the exits. Both of them. In unison. As if they'd been partners for years.

Still crouching, they rushed through the front doors, splitting up when they were outside—Ironman to the right, Klein to the left. They kept to the shadows, checking passersby in an instant, scoping approaching vehicles just as quickly. And then Lyons darted out into the street less than a heartbeat or two after they'd exited the Lucky Dragon. He sent a six-round volley after a big late-model black sedan swerving back and forth down the avenue.

There was a satisfying thud as two of the rounds hit the rear trunk, and then the automobile skidded sideways beneath a streetlight and sped off down a side alley.

"Did you see the license plate?" Klein asked as she caught up to him.

Lyons surveyed the street. Even before he and Haley had exited the restaurant, pedestrians on the sidewalk had dropped to the ground at the first sound of gunshots. Two cars cruising down the block had pulled over at the first sight of muzzle-flashes. "No," he said simply. "It all happened too quickly. You better get back in there and call for some ambulances and—"

"I've already got the headwaiter calling for police and paramedics."

"I'm going to have a talk with some of those people getting up over there. Maybe someone saw a face in that car, or recognized the car itself. Something. Anything."

In the distance the roar of a speeding engine and screeching tires faded on the muggy night breeze.

9

Hear no evil, see no evil, speak no evil.

That was the response Carl Lyons got from the people crouching behind trash cans or parked cars in front of the Lucky Dragon Restaurant—at least from those he could confront. Most darted off down dark alleys or deserted side streets when he approached. No one asked questions in Chinatown. People gossiped and laughed and sometimes they cried. But curiosity had killed more than a few snoops and busybodies in this part of town.

Seven people died at the Lucky Dragon that night. A cloud of guilt hung over both Lyons and Klein as they watched paramedics and assistants from the medical examiner's office body-bag the victims before rolling the gurneys out to the gray meat wagon. Chief of Detectives Crowe showed up. He shook hands with Lyons and acknowledged Klein with a fatherly nod, but dismissed both their suspicions that the shooters had been with the Phi-Chau Gang, out for revenge.

"The Lucky Dragon has been refusing extortion demands for the past several weeks," he revealed. "They're cooperating with us in an investigation involving several area restaurants."

"I knew nothing about that," Klein said.

"Young lady," Crowe said, smiling, "there's a *lot* going on in this town that you and your line cop buddies don't know about. And thank your lucky stars for that. Believe me.''

"Well, I put two hollowpoints into the aluminum ass of that black sedan," Lyons told Crowe.

"Two shots out of six?" Crowe's eyebrows came together in mock shock. "You're losing your touch, Ironman."

"Ironman?" Haley Klein asked, tilting her own head slightly to one side. "Want to explain *that* nickname to me?"

"Forget it," Lyons said, dismissing Crowe's antics with a shrug of his shoulders.

"Forget a moniker like Ironman?" she scoffed. "That's going to be a tall order," Klein answered, standing her ground. "Who the hell tagged you with a handle like Ironman?"

Lyons frowned. "Maybe later. Come on. We've got things to do."

"Keep your nose clean," Crowe warned good-naturedly, knowing the free advice would do the Able Team commando little good.

"Sure," Lyons said, nodding, his mind already on other matters, his eyes seeing things no one else did.

After giving their statements to the responding officers, the two mismatched street partners started back toward One-eyed Ngoc's apartment on foot.

ENGINE RATTLING, tires smoking and the odor of melted-down brakes heavy inside the car, the wiry Vietnamese swerved down another side street and pulled into a dark alleyway.

Sweating profusely, both Vietnamese secret policemen glanced back over their shoulders as a marked SFPD unit raced past, siren screaming and lights flashing. It was evidently on some unrelated emergency call and not after them.

"You okay?" the Asian wearing glasses asked as he glanced over at the driver. His words were in English.

"Yes, but that was close," returned the man sitting behind the steering wheel. His scarred cheek contorted as rivulets of perspiration streamed down from his forehead.

They both turned to stare back at the shattered rear window. "You'd better check the gas tank. Make sure he didn't get that, too," the driver said.

"We're obviously not going up against amateurs in this thing. That was too close back there."

"The policewoman's friend does seem to have a knack for gunplay."

"Did you recognize him?"

"No. But I plan on finding out who he is. The man obviously wants to play rough. And I can definitely accommodate him."

"Do you think perhaps he's one of those crazy American veterans of the 1970s campaign?"

"It's doubtful. But next time around we won't underestimate his abilities—his or the woman's, though she doesn't seem to be very trigger-happy."

"I'll get out and check the gas tank now."

"Yes . . . you do that."

As he emerged from the black sedan and started walking to the rear of the car, Vietnamese Secret Police Captain Chen Chi Vinh felt his shoulders tensing. He half expected the sudden night silence to be shredded by the discharge of a gun. He half expected his companion to shoot him.

But there was no string of gunshots, only the thumping of his own heart against the haphazard rhythm of honking horns several blocks away.

Vinh glanced up at the skyline of countless rooftops rising all around them. An orange crescent moon hung between two buildings. He was reminded of Hanoi, and Haiphong and the Lake of Swords, and he wished so much that he were home in Vietnam, where life was much simpler and his family's water buffalo gave him half the trouble and one-tenth the fright his partner Major Truong provided on a daily basis ever since he'd been assigned to the Vietnamese Association—a covert Vietnamese operation—in America.

Ah, Vietnam. Sweet soil of my ancestors. Someday I will return to you.

Chen Chi Vinh hoped that it wouldn't be in a pine box, his veins filled with the same chemical juice used to preserve frogs, toads and laboratory rats.

VINCENT LU WAS STANDING guard beside his shoeshine box when Carl Lyons and Haley Klein returned to One-eyed Ngoc's apartment house. Officer Klein had only begun to ask Vincent how he was doing when a nearby door flew open and an old mama-san scampered out of a studio unit. She delivered a heated harangue in rapid-fire Chinese at the policewoman, shaking a rigid forefinger in reprimand the entire time, then dragged a shrugging, bored Vincent Lu out of the hallway and into the tiny flat, slamming the door shut again.

"Any idea what *that* was all about?" Klein asked, glancing at Lyons.

"I'd say she was trying to tell you not to involve the kid in what is obviously developing into a serious police matter."

"Well, shit, how do they expect me to save Chinatown if I don't get any cooperation?"

"I believe you said the magic word," Lyons said as he started toward a door on the other side of the hallway.

"The magic word?"

"Chinatown."

"See no evil, hear no evil, speak no evil," Klein said, matching his frown.

"Something like that."

Lyons knocked on the resident's door several times. Receiving no answer, he proceeded to the next one. And the next one. And the next one. The entire floor had obviously overheard the confrontation with Vincent Lu's granny.

"No great loss," Haley decided, abandoning her disappointment. "Vincent might have been the only clue—the only real witness I've had to this point—but even he didn't see anything of real value. The kid only heard a struggle. The bad guys got away down the fire escape."

"Then we're back to square one."

"I'm an optimist."

"And I'm keeping the fingers on my gun hand crossed."

A door at the far end of the hallway—directly across from One-eyed Ngoc's unit—opened for them, however. The woman standing in the dark doorway was in her late fifties and confessed to having spent a few days preparing tea for Old Man Ngoc, a few nights preparing his bed. She willingly invited them into her apartment.

Her skin was dark and marked with liver spots along her sunken cheeks. Her black hair, streaked with gray, was pulled back in a bun and held in place by a long ivory pin. Ever-smiling, she squinted at them through round gold-framed spectacles. She told them her name was Mrs. Pao and that she was a widow for some thirty years now, her husband having been killed by Binh Xuyen river pirates on the Saigon River in the late 1950s.

Her apartment was a cramped studio with no bedroom, only a pullout bed. Grainy black-and-white photos—framed in chrome or brass—decorated all the walls in a cluttered sort of way. Lyons noted that unsmiling people, probably dead ancestors, were portrayed in nearly every one.

"There is not a whole lot I can tell you about Mr. Ngoc," the woman said politely, properly. Clad in a *cheong-sam* that was flashy and colorful, she placed small porcelain cups on the round lacquer-wood table. Her smile concealed the pain of loneliness ruling her life now that Ngoc was gone. "Mr. Ngoc would come by now and then," she continued, "and we would have tea and perhaps play a round of mah-jongg. That was when Mr. Tran was not around, of course."

Haley's eyes lit up. "Mr. Tran?"

"Yes. When Mr. Tran came to call, Mr. Ngoc had to leave and go along with him. It could all be rather disturbing at times."

Lyons was impressed with Mrs. Pao's fluency. "Did either Mr. Ngoc or Mr. Tran have jobs that you were aware of?" he asked.

"Oh, no, no," she said, laughing softly. "I do not think either of them worked. Mr. Ngoc was, perhaps, receiving some assistance from the government. Not welfare. Social security, maybe, though I cannot be sure. He never volunteered such information, and I never asked."

"And Mr. Tran?"

"Mr. Tran was a bit of an oddity. A flashy dresser—a real ladies' man. Yes, always with a pretty young girl on his arm. The dance hall kind. Not common street tramps, but the expensive kind, the type you must telephone to come to your house. Yes, Mr. Tran would come to the building here many times, showing his latest young thing off to Mr. Ngoc. I think Mr. Tran was independently wealthy."

"And Mr. Ngoc?" Haley asked, sensing something Carl didn't pick up on. "How would he react to Mr. Tran's string of pretty female faces?"

"Oh, it would upset Mr. Ngoc sometimes. You see, Mr. Ngoc was not the playboy type. Not like Mr. Tran. No, Mr. Ngoc was very conservative . . . very low-key. He still has a wife back in Vietnam, you know. That's what he told me."

"He told you this?" Lyons asked.

"Yes. He said he spent all his savings and all the money he could earn at the gambling dens and sent it back to Vietnam, to his wife in Saigon, trying to get her out. He was a very depressed man, from what I could see. Poor, poor Mr. Ngoc. He told me his wife tried to escape by boat nine times! Can you imagine that? Nine! And caught by the Communists every single time! Poor, poor Mrs. Ngoc. By the time she gets out—by the time the Communists are finished with her—she will be a pitiful thing.''

"What about the disappearances of Mr. Ngoc and Mr. Tran?'' Haley asked, trying to get back to the problem at hand. "Do you have any theories?''

"Disappeared? Have they not just gone off on a bus tour to Las Vegas?'' she replied.

"Las Vegas?''

"Yes. They usually went about once every five or six weeks. Always lost money, but they returned looking younger than when they left, and Mr. Ngoc would not talk to me for days afterward. I think he was feeling guilty.''

"Feeling guilty?''

"Of the golden-haired *gwai-loh* girls they met there. In Las Vegas. Showgirls. As I was saying, Mr. Tran was always bragging about his female conquests, and promising to 'set up' Mr. Ngoc. Is that how you say it?''

"Yes,'' Lyons said, thinking of a different type of setup, and just who exactly might be behind it.

"Well, as I said, I'm hoping they just went on a tour to Las Vegas, but in my heart I fear they may have been victims of foul play.''

"And why do you think that?'' Klein asked.

"Like young Vincent Lu, I, too, heard the scream of terror coming from Mr. Ngoc's room that night.''

"But you saw nothing?'' Lyons asked. "No one suspicious?''

"I must confess to you that I was too frightened to leave my apartment and, as you can see, I cannot afford a telephone. But, no, through my peephole in the door there, I saw no one in the hallway. No one coming, no one going.''

As Lyons and Klein glanced over at the door Mrs. Pao was gesturing to, they heard the creaking of floorboards in the hallway directly outside. The footsteps seemed to stop directly outside the door.

Instinctively Lyons's hand reached in to rest on the handle of the revolver hidden beneath his jean jacket. "You two get behind the—" he started to say when the front door's top and bottom hinges were blown off.

A burst of green tracers danced across the floor toward them as the loose door—blown from its hinges and airborne now—flew inward through the tiny studio apartment. Lyons watched the rounds stitch several planks between him and Haley without hitting anyone. There were no ricochets. In the apartment below someone started screaming hysterically.

In the hallway outside two Asian men brandishing AK-47s charged in yelling Vietcong war cries.

10

Carl Lyons's revolver had hardly cleared leather when Haley Klein began blasting away with her off-duty snub-nosed .38. The pistol had only a five-shot capacity, but that seemed to be enough.

After firing off his thirty-round burst, the grim-faced Asian in front paused to reload his AK with another banana clip while his companion—a bespectacled, almost scholarly-looking man—stepped forward to stop the first three bullets from Klein's pistol. All three of them slammed into his midsection, doubling him over with a hideous scream.

Klein's fourth shot struck the scar-faced gunman in the thigh, whirling him around, and he stumbled back out into the hallway out of sight. Klein's fifth bullet split a door frame on the other side of the hallway.

"Fantastic!" Lyons yelled over at her as he jumped onto Vietnamese Secret Police Captain Chen Chi Vinh and wrestled the automatic rifle away from him. It wasn't much of a fight—the Vietnamese was already going into shock from the pain of three belly wounds.

"What about that other guy?" the policewoman demanded as trembling fingers struggled to force five fresh cartridges into the warm cylinder. It was almost as if the shells were too large to fit smoothly into the tiny cylinder slots. She felt her chest heaving, her temples pulsing, the rush of excitement and fear making her nearly drunk on adrenaline.

They could both hear someone stumbling down the hallway toward the stairwell, abandoning the fight.

Lyons cautiously peered out through the apartment doorway, but there were no other shooters waiting for him outside. "I'm going after him," he told her. "You keep an eye on *this* clown."

"I'll call for an ambulance," she replied.

Lyons fished through an inner pocket of his jean jacket and produced a business card with nothing on it but an eleven-digit phone number. "Call this number first!" he instructed. The look in his eyes left no room for argument. "Ask for Hal. Tell him you're calling for Ironman. Brief him on what just went down here!" he finished as he started into the hallway.

"*Then* can I call my own people?" Klein asked, immediately angry with herself for allowing this stranger to take command of the situation.

But Lyons didn't respond. She listened to his footsteps rushing down the hallway, and the stairwell door slamming shut behind him.

Klein's shadow fell over Chen. She was careful to keep the pistol barrel trained between his closed eyes. She'd heard war stories about the VC. They had the personality of a snake—the cunning of a panther on the prowl.

Chen groaned, rolled slowly to one side, then the other. Suddenly—but even more slowly—he reached up to her, his eyes still tightly closed, and groaned again.

Klein stepped back gingerly out of the gunman's reach. "Consider yourself under arrest," she said through gritted teeth, feeling good about the shooting, feeling great about her own actions. "Make another move like that and I'll cancel your ticket, for good, buster."

"Help me." Chen's eyes opened only slightly as he continued to reach out for her before he dropped back into semiconsciousness.

Feeling the postshooting letdown that most officers didn't experience for hours—or days—afterward, Klein holstered her .38 and began looking for a telephone. Then she remembered that Mrs. Pao couldn't afford one.

Klein found herself thinking about her old Air Force days. Should I abandon my post? Should I take the initiative and seek a higher authority, use my head and adapt to the developing situation, a potentially explosive situation? She wished she was back at Lowry, where everything had always been so simple and orderly, so cut and dried, so black and white....

Or had it?

"Do you think any of your neighbors might have a phone I could borrow?" she asked as she turned toward the studio flat's lone tenant.

But Mrs. Pao was no longer in a talkative mood. Eyes wide and bulging, but unblinking, she sat on her haunches, propped against the balcony's blood-smeared and spider-webbed sliding glass doors, a solitary bluish-purple entry wound in the center of her forehead.

THE MOMENT HE ENTERED the concrete stairwell Lyons could tell his prey had headed for the roof. The man's footfalls filled the chamber like echoes in an elevator shaft.

Releasing his .357's hammer from single action back to the less dangerous double action, Lyons climbed the concrete steps, following the blood trail left behind by his quarry.

A rooftop foot chase. It was coming. He could sense it. And Carl Lyons loved skyline pursuits above a big-city panorama! As he raced up the steps in total silence, catlike, using only the balls of his feet, Ironman briefly flashed back to his days with LAPD, and the hundred or so rooftop foot chases he'd been involved in. Atop the world like that, death lurked behind each chimney, each ventilation duct, every air shaft. At night TV antennae and their guy wires could trip you up, send you tumbling out over the edge into space, into the black, bottomless pit of sudden nothingness, the deep, endless sleep. He'd had partners who had screwed up, taken the plunge. One had survived. Survived to collect his fifty percent pension from a medical discharge—but never to walk again.

All these thoughts raced through Carl Lyons's head as he slowly, silently, lifted the trapdoor that gave access to the rooftop.

A cool breeze immediately enveloped him, cloaked his limbs, captured him in a mind-altering trance, however elusive, however fleeting. He'd experienced the sensation before: Lyons was eight floors above the street now. Above the ground-clinging layer of smog and noise and everyday tensions. That accounted for it. That and the adrenaline rush.

He was in another world now, a surreal world, a dangerous land of unseen demons and lurking death. But Lyons knew that, with .45 in hand, he was master of all he surveyed. That was the way it had to be if he was to win tonight.

The Able Team commando's thumb pulled the pistol's hammer slowly back again until it locked into its sensitive single-action mode.

He glanced to the left, then to the right. Nothing. A blanket of darkness. Above, that brilliant, ever-present display of uncaring stars stretching out over the ocean, beckoning him, teasing.

He forced himself to concentrate. This was no game. This was life or death, with brainless firearms controlled by two warriors from different worlds the only judge and jury. An hour from now he could be cold meat on some irritated coroner's morgue table.

"Damn," he muttered to himself, willing his senses sharp again. "Damn." Must concentrate. Must kill him. Him or me. And I'm the better soldier.

He prowled the rooftop's edge in both directions. Briefly his eyes darted in the direction of the next building, but his target hadn't had enough time to escape via that route, and the distance between tenements was too great, anyway. His target had a leg wound, but where was the blood trail?

Gun arm extended, pistol swinging back and forth, he prowled the darkness, footstep by footstep, concentrating on every protruding shape, every out-of-place object. Out of place down in the real world, perhaps, but not up here, Ironman, he mentally reprimanded himself.

Something seemed to roll, bounce, then scamper through the steam clinging to the roofline's edge in the distance, but he held off firing at the last moment. Rats. Three rats, chased by a tomcat.

A muted sigh of relief left his lungs, and he started to turn in the opposite direction when the gun barrel came up hard against the base of his skull.

Lyons was a tough man. He'd fought bigger, meaner brawlers the world over, and still managed to come out on top somehow. But tonight his knees were giving out. He felt bolts of pain lance through both temples, lifting him free of gravitational pull, floating him above it all—his world, his worries, his cares.

But then, quite suddenly, Lyons's world was racing back up to meet him head-on, and the rooftop slammed against his face, knocking his head back, rolling his eyeballs up into his brain, where thoughts scattered in terror and his mind tumbled head over heels into the black abyss.

HALEY KLEIN'S CALL to Stony Man Farm was electronically relayed, without delay, to the command post Hal Brognola had set up in a back office of the San Francisco Police Department's detective division. Blancanales and

Schwarz were both sitting at the table, going over SFPD stat reports when it rang.

Gadgets picked up the receiver. "Sixty-eight, thirty-two," he said, giving the last four digits of the phone number. "State your piece, brother."

"This is Officer Klein, SFPD," Haley said. "I'm calling for Ironman."

"Go ahead, ma'am," Schwarz said, his pen tapping a notepad nervously.

Klein gave the street address of the apartment building. "We've just had a shooting situation at this location. One bad guy down and out. The other topside."

"Topside?"

"On the roof. Ironman went after him."

"Is he armed?"

"AK-47," she replied quickly. "They both had AKs."

"Does Ironman have any backup?"

"No!" she yelled, beginning to lose her patience fast. "He's on his own! Now would you guys get somebody over here to—"

"We're on our way! What apartment you in?" Schwarz demanded.

"I'm not sure!" Klein glanced at the bullet-riddled door lying just inside the apartment across the hallway, but the number was on the other side and had probably been destroyed, anyway. "But we're on the seventh floor. You can't miss us!" she added sarcastically. "Just follow the smell of gunsmoke!"

"We're on our way!"

THAT VIETNAMESE SECRET POLICE Major Truong didn't immediately dispose of Carl Lyons after pistol-whipping him unconscious from behind could probably be attributed to Truong's fear that the diary he'd plucked from Ironman's back pocket might not answer all his questions about Tran Van Thieu and Ngoc Ung Mau's recent activities.

Truong might have to twist the American's arm a little bit before he killed him.

In his waistband Truong kept Lyons's Colt Python safely within easy reach while he thumbed through the diary.

Lying facedown against the roof's harsh gravel coating, Lyons quickly regained consciousness. Remaining in top physical condition and participating in an almost daily regimen of rigorous workouts with his fellow Able Team commandos took half the credit. The other fifty percent had something to do with the will to live, and Ironman's never-say-die, nut-up-and-do-it attitude.

His right eye slowly opened, and Lyons realized he was facedown on a rooftop overlooking Chinatown. Almost immediately he recalled the firecracker string of events leading up to this present, less-than-desirable situation. The cool Bay breeze caressed an aching head and face. His eyeball rotated slowly, trying to pinpoint the sound of fluttering pages.

He knew the gunman—the AK-armed Asian he was chasing—had relieved him of the pocket diary. Now he had two tasks to perform: determine the shooter's exact spot in relation to his own, and retrieve the small .380 auto from its hidden ankle holster affixed with Velcro straps to his calf.

Wondering how bad the shooter's thigh wound was, Lyons began planning. He wouldn't have much more time. He wondered how long he'd been out, how long they'd been up here together on the rooftop, sharing the night breeze.

Not too long, surely. Klein would have phoned for assistance. Then he remembered Mrs. Pao saying she had no phone. Perhaps the gut-shot gunman was doped up, and Haley was wrestling with him even now, losing the fight, losing her gun, losing her life. Perhaps the man was dead, and Haley had persuaded one of the neighbors to let her use the phone.

Ears cocked, Lyons listened for the sound of distant sirens growing nearer. But there were none. Only a far-off, lonely train whistle. As a child, train whistles had always made him long for adventure, for travel to faraway lands, distant ground. He couldn't grow up fast enough back then. Now he found himself wishing he'd chosen a safe clerk's career somewhere.

Had Haley gotten through to Brognola and the team? Maybe they hadn't made it to San Francisco. Surely Hal would have uniformed assistance rushing to help him at that very moment, though!

It had to be now, or he might forever be the sole occupant of a government-financed pine box. No more waiting, no patient game-playing, waiting for cover to arrive. Tonight there would be no cavalry. He was on his own. That was how he had to play it.

Lyons saw himself in the uniform of a Los Angeles police officer, sitting at a doughnut shop counter with six or seven of his LAPD buddies at 4:30 a.m., critiquing that evening's string of shoot-outs. Critiquing and laughing and bullshitting and bragging, and laughing some more. Always laughing along with the other guy's black humor or grim cynicism. God, he missed the camaraderie. He knew that, somewhere nearby, there were two or three black-and-white units from San Francisco's finest engaging in the same shoptalk. Cops. He missed them. Wished he was sitting between two men in blue, maybe even rubbing shoulders with a policewoman. Hell, he could adjust. As long as she pulled her own weight. Like Klein.

Haley. He saw her face replace that of his old LAPD partner's, and he wondered if he would ever see either person again. Or would he be staring down at a PD-blue crowd as countless uniforms gathered at his funeral and he watched from above, sitting on the edge of some silvery cloud, his personal piece of heavenly real estate.

Angry with his aimless thoughts, he let out a war cry not unlike those the two intruders had given before the shooting had started downstairs. Curled up in the fetal position, making himself as small a target as possible as he reached for and drew the .380 automatic, he kicked out blindly in the direction he sensed his captor to be standing.

Seams along his trousers' lower pant leg split as he struggled to get the pistol out, and then he was firing even before he'd properly positioned the damn thing in the palm of his hand. Two bullets flew past Truong's startled face on either side. A third tore the diary out of his hands and flung it toward the rooftop's edge.

Slack-jawed, the Communist spun around, cried out as his wounded thigh gave him some unexpected pain and started to bring up his rifle, which had been casually balanced across one arm.

Five more rapidly fired shots erupted from the .380 in Lyons's hand, and four of the small slugs danced along the assault rifle's stock, splitting off a large sliver of polished hardwood.

Lyons ignored the voice in his head, screaming to take prisoners. He was mad and he wanted revenge. He wanted this man's head! Several more shots flew from the .380, but unceasing pain was pressing against his temples on both sides like a set of vise grips, and the rounds all traveled high, ascending in a lazy, unseen arc out over the perilous drop between buildings. Then the .380's firing pin slammed forward against an empty chamber, sounding like a sick parakeet's chirp.

"Damn it!" he said, rolling behind a ventilation shaft, well aware he carried no extra clips for the backup automatic. But his target was running off into the darkness, back toward the stairwell, and he'd dropped Lyons's Magnum and the diary, as well.

Feeling dizzy and sick, Ironman staggered over to the stairwell, but his rooftop opponent had vanished. After collecting his wits, the Able Team warrior rushed to the nearest roofline. He stared down at the street eight flights below, but no one darted or limped or crawled off down a nearby alley. He waited a few moments, then staggered across to the opposite edge of the roof, but from this point, too, he couldn't spot the Asian escaping.

Perhaps the gunman had an apartment right here in this very building. But Lyons doubted that. Perhaps Ironman had imagined the whole episode: the shoot-out, ascending to the roof, being clubbed from behind. No, his head ached too much for it to have been any lapse in memory, judgment or sanity.

He scooped up two dark objects lying a few feet away: his Colt Python and Tran Van Thieu's diary. "Damn it," he muttered under his breath, finally heading for the stairwell. "The guys are never gonna let me live this one down."

Two San Francisco police officers were standing in Mrs. Pao's doorway when he reached the seventh level again. Hands on their holstered guns, they glanced warily at Ironman as he approached. But Haley Klein was quick to speak up for Lyons. "He's okay!" she said, putting them at ease. "He's with me!"

"That guy going to make it?" Lyons asked, motioning toward the gunshot victim. In his late forties, the Asian wore an innocent, almost boyish expression. He appeared to be out cold, but the edges of his lips still seemed to be twisted up in a sardonic grin.

"I don't think so." Klein was down on one knee, holding a pressure bandage against the discolored loops of intestine trying to force their way out between her fingers. When he fell, the Asian's belly had ripped open where all three bullet holes formed a straight horizontal shot grouping.

"Detach at perforation," one of the patrolmen, a stocky silver-haired field training officer in his early fifties, muttered with a chilling chuckle.

"What's the ETA on those damn paramedics?" Klein asked him.

"Zero-five," the grizzled old street veteran replied. "Why? Does it really matter?"

"It matters to me!" Klein replied angrily.

"We need him alive," Lyons explained as he brushed between the two officers. "We need answers, or this Chinatown mess might never get unraveled."

"Ain't that the truth." But the officer was still smiling. He didn't care. This was Chinatown. Too many mysteries floating in and out of the back alleys and side streets already. Hell, if he wanted a good detective yarn, he'd wait till he got home to read a Joseph Wambaugh novel.

As Ironman examined the bullet hole in the diary a few minutes later, he wondered how much the intruder had read or remembered while Lyons had lain facedown on the harsh roof gravel, semiconscious and uncomprehending.

He glanced out the open balcony. In the street below, a lone siren was winding down. It wasn't the modern electronic yelp the SFPD units were equipped with, but an old-style fire department contraption. The paramedics had arrived.

"Too late," Klein muttered. She lifted her blood-caked hand from an unmoving corpse. Bright streaks of crimson no longer pulsed from the ghastly wound, no longer oozed from the Asian's shredded belly.

"Any ID?" the patrolman asked. He refused to leave the security of his post at the doorway—from there he was safe from paperwork and would only have to guard the crime scene, at worst, not actually pull out a pen to write a report.

"You know we're not supposed to mess with a shooting victim's personal belongings until the coroner gets here," his partner, a young, idealistic rookie, reminded the FTO. He risked the verbal reprimand only because he was nearing the end of his probationary period. But the street vet pounced anyway.

"Don't second-guess me, son! Now help the lady there check our dead friend here for ID. You got that?"

Vietnamese Secret Police Captain Chen Chi Vinh was carrying no identification tonight, however. Not even one of the phony California driver's licenses Major Truong had acquired for both of them. Tonight he was just John Doe. Another nameless face in the cold, uncaring city of anonymity.

11

"Bi Mat Nguoi Tham Tu."

"What?" Gadgets Schwarz and Carl Lyons both asked Pol Blancanales several hours later as they stood deep inside the bowels of the county morgue, viewing an autopsy on the body of the man Haley Klein had shot with her snubnosed .38.

"The tattoo on his left shoulder there. It's the insignia of a special branch of the Vietnamese Secret Police," Blancanales explained. The men zeroed in on the crossed machetes superimposed over a combination yellow five-pointed star and Soviet sickle.

"You're sure?" Lyons asked.

"The only reason I know about it is because my old Black Beret unit once ambushed a sampan full of the suckers."

Lyons glanced over at Haley Klein as the assistant medical examiner began using a huge set of metal shears to open up John Doe's torso from crotch to throat. "Appears to be three entry wounds along the lower abdominal cavity," the assistant coroner said into a tape recorder mike suspended from the ceiling directly over the morgue table. "From a small-caliber firearm in a horizontal pattern, beginning eight inches in from the right hip, proceeding..."

Lyons tried to gauge the expression on Klein's face: was it unabashed pride in her accomplishment, or horror at what she had done down in Chinatown? He simply couldn't read her features. Ironman shrugged as the assistant coroner began describing the belly wounds in depth. The important thing was that Haley had come through for him when it had counted most. She'd proven herself in her own eyes. And that was what was important, what counted most.

Carl Lyons had never doubted her.

When they first arrived at the morgue, a group of police officers assigned to work Fisherman's Wharf had congregated outside the lab. Lyons had overheard them talking about a severed head they'd just brought in from one of the dock units, where it had been discovered in the back of a garbage truck.

"Gave one of the garbagemen quite a fright," the patrolman telling the story had said, erupting into a long, drawn-out bellow.

"The other garbageman, he said it weren't no big thing," another officer had added to the story. "Claimed he'd seen it all. Said it was his third severed head this year. Yep, that's what he said! I swear it."

The morgue lobby had erupted into hearty bellows again. "You'd have thought we was woi'kin' the South Bronx or somet'ing!" a third line cop had said in a grating Brooklyn accent.

"She was a pretty thing, she was! Asian or something!"

"Or something!"

"Yeah!" And they had all exploded again.

After the autopsy, Lyons gave the assistant coroner a sealed document. "This is where the body goes," he ordered. "No place else."

"Well, I'll have to clear it with my—"

"You clear it with the White House, if you have to clear it with anyone," Lyons said, silencing him with steel-blue eyes.

"Yeah, sure," the man muttered. He loved a good argument now and then, but he was getting too old to fight. "Screw it, anyway."

"Appreciate it, Pops," Ironman said, his features softening.

"Yeah, right!" the coroner said, waving him off. "Fine, fine. Now just get the hell out of my little house of horrors, okay? *Whoever* the hell you guys are!"

USING THE DIARY DIAGRAMS retrieved from Tran Van Thieu's apartment, and sophisticated electronic gear he'd brought along from the Farm, Gadgets Schwarz took only three hours to locate One-eyed Ngoc's scroll and its List of Fourteen, secreted behind a wall of bricks in a sealed-off section of subway tunnels beneath the city of San Francisco.

"And what do we have here?" Blancanales said, his eyes lighting up as Gadgets, standing on a pile of cinder blocks, handed the plastic tube down to Ironman.

"Be careful," Haley cautioned. "It might be booby-trapped or something."

Lyons peered at it from several angles. "It's not heavy enough to be a pipe bomb," he decided. "And there's no uneven distribution of weight, like you'd find with C-4 plastique, or even a nitro charge. No, there's just a note or something in here." He began unscrewing the cap at one end. "A note...or nothing." But then he slid out a rolled-up scroll that was withered and yellowed and looked older than the four of them combined.

"What does it say?" Haley asked.

"It doesn't say anything," Ironman answered, holding it out for them all to see. "It's a list. Fourteen cities. All stateside. Nothing more." He flipped the scroll over, but it was blank on the reverse. "Nothing less."

"Truly bizarre," Blancanales said, frowning. "All this gunplay you've told us about, and for what? A list of fourteen cities? Hell, an almanac would have come cheaper."

"Nothing's ever as simple or meaningless as it may seem at first to be, Rosario," Gadgets said, grinning as he inserted the protruding lens of a bulky, generatorlike device up against the dark crevice and snapped off a flash.

On the hidden ledge where the plastic tube had been resting, nothing *was* as it seemed, for, utilizing the portable equivalent of a much larger X-ray machine, Able Team's science wizard was able to detect a depression in the dust. Two initials: S&W.

"The same initials drawn into the diary diagram here," Lyons pointed out.

"Smith & Wesson," Gadgets said quickly.

"What?" Both Lyons and Klein leaned closer to the photograph Schwarz had taken of the interior crevice.

"See this smooth depression, and this jagged one?" Schwarz asked, running his finger along the snapshot's grainy features. "Barrel and pistol grip."

"A Smith & Wesson .357 Magnum?" Klein suggested.

"No," Schwarz said, shaking his head. "Smaller. "A .38 Special. Four-inch barrel, or maybe a snub-nose like yours. The dust here was disturbed, so I can't tell the exact barrel length."

"But why would someone remove the pistol and not the scroll?" Lyons asked. "He—or she—was obviously keeping the gun here for insurance."

"So many questions, and no answers," Schwarz said, laughing with intrigue. "Here! Let me see that list."

As the sounds indigenous to a big city's underworld catacombs created a backdrop of eerie noises, Schwarz's narrowed eyes scanned the list once, twice, then a third time.

"Anything strike a chord with you?" Schwarz asked Blancanales.

"Negative," Pol answered as he read and reread the fourteen city names listed.

"How 'bout you, Ironman?"

"No," Lyons said, shaking his head as he examined the list. "Nothing."

"Let me see that sucker," Haley Klein said, grabbing the brittle scroll and shining her flashlight on it.

"Truly bizarre," Blancanales said, nodding his head again. He glanced over at Lyons, then Klein. "Any idea what we're supposed to get from these names? Either of you two?"

"Don't look at me," Lyons said, walking away toward a construction ledge that overlooked an abandoned subway platform. Rats scampered off at his approach.

"Well, it's just that you guys have been in on this fiasco from the start. Me and Gadgets here, we're just starting to get our feet wet, amigo."

"Yeah, sorry," Ironman said, sighing.

"None of those cities mean anything to me," Klein told Politician. "I've never even heard of any of them except Ventura and Westminster, the two in California."

"So what do we do now?" Schwarz asked as he began folding up his equipment and squeezing it into a portable but bulky suitcase.

"We check 'em out," Lyons said.

Blancanales held the scroll out. "The addresses listed in these fourteen separate cities?"

"Every last one of them," Ironman said. "Beginning with Ventura, California. It's the closest one."

"This is the pits," Haley complained as she stared at a large snake slithering off through the shadows. "I want to go home," she purred like a schoolgirl, hoping to get a laugh.

The attempt failed miserably.

"The address on Moran Street in Westminster," Lyons said, gently shaking his head as if deciding whether to proceed into a lion's den unarmed. "It's in the heart of Little Saigon."

"Aw, shit," Blancanales muttered, his eyeballs rolling toward the tunnel's lizard-infested ceiling. "I hate Little Saigon."

"Something tells me we're in for a world of hurt," Gadgets mumbled uneasily. "Again."

THE ADDRESS ON VENTURA'S stretch of Pacific Coast Highway was occupied by a lone structure—the Clifftop Hotel. It was a recently renovated, twenty-unit building—formerly a two-story wooden Army barracks painted mint-green—that sat atop a cliff overlooking the Pacific Ocean. The owner had had it repainted an off-white shade in hopes of matching the mollusks and cockleshells that washed up on shore after each evening's high tide.

The beach was less than a hundred yards away, at the bottom of a steep hill that wasn't really a cliff at all, but *was* quite precarious to negotiate on foot due to the giant rocks deposited haphazardly by nature from the surf line up to the hillside's midway point. The rocks took on weird, almost frightening shapes after twilight, but were obviously nothing more than monstrous chunks of immovable stone by day.

Able Team spent a good six hours scouring the rocks that following morning, but they found nothing that could possibly be construed as bringing them any closer to the ten million dollars worth of emeralds, or the missing documents.

In a silver four-door Plymouth, borrowed from the San Francisco PD detective bureau, they'd driven the four hundred and fifty miles south from the Bay Area to L.A. County's western edge in under nine hours, overnight.

At dawn they'd had breakfast at a modest eatery attached to the hotel. They didn't actually check into the Clifftop. Instead, as the morning progressed, and tourists began arriving—making the three grim-faced men and the blond beauty less conspicuous—they inspected certain portions of the hotel itself without trying to appear overly obvious. They eyeballed the gift shop, dining facility and main lounge area, for instance...all places open to the general public. But again nothing earth-shattering made itself known to them.

Schwarz was assigned to browse through the few objects of art on display, mostly urns and frontier statues of little value, while Blancanales examined the dozens of paintings hanging on the lobby walls. Again no clues burst forth.

Lyons was of the opinion that none were lying in wait, or hiding from them, either. "This is a bust," he finally said as sunset approached. "There's nothing here to lead us anywhere. It's a goddamn wild-goose chase. And I have no intention of hopping all over the friggin' countryside checking out every address on that stupid scroll. It would be nothing but a waste of time. We'd stand a better chance returning to Chinatown and beginning at square one."

"Maybe. Maybe not," Blancanales said, scratching at the stubble on his chin in thought. "That brochure in the lobby said this place recently underwent a renovation, right?"

"Yeah, so what?"

"Let's have a little talk with management."

The hotel owner told them that the only thing to be removed during the renovation the winter before was a wishing well in the rear sun deck area, overlooking the ocean. "Yes," he told them. "It was there a good fifty years. Long before *I* ever came along."

"Why did you remove the wishing well?" Lyons inquired.

"Actually, it was getting to be quite an eyesore," the hotel owner said. "People weren't only throwing pennies and nickels, dimes and quarters into the damn thing, but filling it up with trash, empty cans and bottles and the like, when no one was looking. I just don't know what humanity's coming to anymore these days! And water, well, water's damn expensive, you know? Even this close to the sea. So we just decided to shut it down. It was an albatross, a dinosaur on the verge of extinction. I think the original designer was trying to build what was supposed to be an actual drinking well. We finally just had it torn down and hauled away. Filled the hole up too, clean to the top.''

"Do you remember if they found anything at the bottom of the well?'' Schwarz asked, not knowing exactly what they were looking for. "Anything at all?''

"Anything *strange*?'' Klein added.

"Oh, there was an old rusty tin container. Looked like a child's lunch box, with Disneyland designs all over it.''

"Disneyland designs?'' Blancanales asked.

"You know—submariners exploring a thousand fathoms under the sea. That kind of stuff.''

"Did anyone open the lunch box up?'' Klein asked.

"Naw,'' the hotel owner said. "It was dripping with rusty water and long strands of seaweed. The workmen just trashed it along with the other stuff.''

"Without opening it?'' Lyons asked.

"Right.''

"Any idea where they took the debris?'' Blancanales asked, his eyes routinely scanning the coastline highway up above and coming to rest on a black sedan sitting by itself at a rest stop.

"Who knows?'' the owner said, laughing bitterly. "They're supposed to haul that kind of crap to a landfill over near Santa Barbara, but you know they never do. Probably took it out on a barge and dumped it at sea. This planet's dying, you know. Pollution everywhere. Rain forests shrinking. Now they say the ozone's going. Before you know it, all the artesian drilling they're doing underground is gonna get a mother nature backlash in the form of volcanoes pushing up right through the center of Beverly Hills. Mark my words!''

"Santa Barbara?'' Lyons said, exchanging unenthusiastic looks with his cohorts. He, too, had spotted the car a hundred yards away, and it was beginning to look more and more like the sedan he'd put two bullets into back in Chinatown.

Haley was the first to speak out against the look in his eyes. "I'm not trudging knee-high through a dump, looking for a kid's lunch box that probably doesn't have a damn thing inside it, gentlemen."

She sounded adamant.

12

The second address on the List of Fourteen belonged to a tiny gift shop in the heart of Orange County's Little Saigon, a three-hour drive to the southeast, following the coastline. It was a tiny one-story cubbyhole in a long, nondescript row of similar cubbyholes that ran down off Bolsa Avenue, the main drag.

The shop had a giant purple dragon in the front plate-glass window. The words emblazoned across the creature's fire-breathing snout proclaimed: Dragon's Tooth Gift Shop.

Inside, one passed a cashier's cubicle on the left immediately upon entering the store. Directly ahead, in the central section of the shop, Chinese and Vietnamese videocassettes, mostly epic soap operas with a nineteenth-century warrior theme to them, were piled from floor to ceiling in a pyramidlike display.

Racks along the left wall held key chains, lapel pins and desktop flag sets in plastic packets, all bearing the gold South Vietnamese flag with its three bloodred horizontal stripes. Hanging from the far wall were tapestries and lacquer-wood paintings, some made in Asia, some in Little Saigon.

As Lyons's people entered the Dragon's Tooth, they nodded to the proprietor—a young, attractive woman in her late teens or early twenties—and spread out. Gadgets headed directly for the videocassettes, in search of some obscure clue. Ironman began a countergrid tour of the entire shop, beginning with the key chains and lapel pins, and working his way past the art objects over the book racks.

Haley remained slightly inside the door, watching the street outside. The black sedan that had been spotted parked on a stretch of coastal highway overlooking the Clifftop Hotel hadn't been seen again, but Lyons maintained he had a gut feeling about the car, and that the feeling was a bad one.

Moran Street, unlike the much more congested Bolsa Strip, was a narrow two-lane roadway with little traffic on it other than commercial deliveries and pickups. The men of Able Team had learned long ago, however, that their gut feelings usually paid off.

If the old instincts kicked in, post a guard.

Blancanales went straight to the cashier, of course. He had an image to uphold, for Rosario was a legend in his own mind. A legend with the ladies.

She was tall for a Vietnamese—at least five-seven—and her hair, jet-black and straight, fell to her waist. She wore the traditional Vietnamese gossamer-thin, form-hugging *ao dai* gown—in this case a flowing royal blue tunic that dropped to her ankles. It was closed at the throat yet slit along the sides and was worn over billowing black pantaloons.

"May I help you?" she asked in unaccented English, batting the long lashes of her dark almond eyes.

Blancanales was impressed by her high cheekbones and finely chiseled nose. Either she was Eurasian—a French-Vietnamese mix—or a member of that rare Hue elite, the royal family line guarded for thousands of years at the Imperial City, north of Old Saigon.

He almost had to shake his head to break the trance. "Mr. Ngoc," he said quickly, wondering where the words had come from, how any thoughts at all could be generated in the presence of such extreme beauty. "Mr. Ngoc and Mr. Tran," he said, groping, hoping against hope for some flicker of recognition in her eyes, some sign of deception in her features, even if she said what he knew—what they all knew—she would say. "Have they been around lately?"

"I'm afraid I don't know either man," she replied casually, eyes dueling with his, yet facial expression cold, noncommittal. "Do they live around here?" she asked, pausing to gauge the expressions on his friends' faces. "Perhaps they would know my father," she said, staring long and hard at Haley's blond locks, then glancing away, upper lip curling slightly in a show of emotion Politician couldn't read. Was it envy? Or disgust?

"No," Pol said. "No, I don't think so. Nice place you've got here."

"It pays for itself. This is our fourteenth year," she said proudly as she began stacking Vietnamese music cassettes beside the cash register. "We left Saigon in 1975, three days before the fall. Are you and your friends police?"

"Uh, no, not at all," Schwarz said, joining Blancanales. "Just . . . just tourists."

"Sure," the cashier said, smiling for the first time, but it was a cynical smile. "And I'm Madonna."

Lyons pressed against the counter between them. "Nothing," he told Gadgets and Pol. His eyes shifted to inspect the woman's features. "Mind if we take a look in the back room?" he asked.

"Back room?" she echoed, laughing softly. "You guys *are* cops." But the possibility didn't seem to bother her.

"We're not," Haley argued as she stepped away from the door. "We're . . . P.I.s."

"P.I.s?" the cashier queried as Lyons's eyeballs rolled toward the ceiling.

"Private investigators," Haley explained.

"Mind if we have a look?" Lyons asked again.

"There *is* no back room," the cashier said, holding her hands out in resignation. "You're looking at the whole shop."

Slowly, as if drawn to it by some supernatural power, Lyons's eyes rose above the cashier's head and came to rest on a brightly painted statue. It was a porcelain dancer, nude save for a strip of ornamental beads modestly cloaking portions of the smooth pelvis. She squatted with bent knees, hands clasped in front of her face, a spired headdress rising over her brow. From bright crimson toenails to the golden tip of the spire, she stood about three feet high. The shopkeeper kept her displayed on a shelf protruding from the wall behind the cashier's station. Her breasts jutted out proudly at Ironman, her turquoise eyes—precious stones of some sort—seemed to follow his every move.

Lyons's expression was quite obvious, and the cashier quickly read the look in his eyes. "I'm sorry, sir, the statue's not for sale. It has . . . sentimental value to my father."

"Oh?" Blancanales questioned as he moved beside Carl.

"My eldest brother rescued it from a temple that was being looted at Angkor Wat in Cambodia back in 1968. The Khmers stole it from the Thais, of course, hundreds of years earlier."

"It must be worth a pretty penny," Gadgets Schwarz said, reaching up and running his fingers along the statue's amber thighs.

"There is nothing unique about it," the woman replied. "It's just a statue."

"A collector's piece perhaps?" Blancanales asked.

"No. Just a very old statue." The slightest hint of irritation was finally creeping into the pretty woman's tone. "A cheap, somewhat erotic statue, nothing else, but it's the one thing my brother presented to my father. There's no other reminder that my eldest brother ever walked this earth— nothing but the twinkle in this naked lady's glass eyes.

"My brother was killed during the fall of Saigon, trying to help get our family onto one of the boats. Some *cao boi* shot him in the back, then disappeared into the mobs onshore. I never saw the gunman's face, or I promise you, I would have remained behind, searching, until I found the man and made him pay."

"I believe you would have done just that," Lyons said, feeling a chill swirl up and down his spine at the thought that such a dainty, unassuming woman could radiate such hate, such determination. Ironman stared at a tiny placard of gold leaf hanging on a string of wire around the dancer's neck. Resting against her throat were three numbers—714—engraved on the quarter-inch square of precious metal. "Any idea what the number means?" he asked her.

"They are my father's lucky numbers—seven and fourteen. And his father's before him. My eldest brother's also, but now he's dead. The numbers weren't lucky enough."

"Perhaps luck is how we read the cards of fate," Lyons said, and Blancanales and Schwarz exchanged uneasy glances. "*You* survived the fall of Saigon, as did most of your family. Your father, by the way, I'd like to meet him. What's his name?"

"Our family surname is Pham. My father has several first names—Dai-Ton among them—but everybody just calls him the General. I'm afraid he's somewhat of a political activist, though."

"Oh?" Lyons said.

"Yes. I'm hoping he'll soon forget it. He spends more time at the *pho* restaurants up on Bolsa, associating with veterans of the Old Saigon regime, than here at the shop. Face, you know. He's always trying to prevent loss of face. Many of the ARVNs—"

"Former South Vietnamese soldiers," Blancanales said.

"Yes," she said, nodding gracefully. "Many of them still feel intense guilt over the loss of our country to the Communists fifteen years ago. My father has taken it upon himself to convince everyone that the spineless politicians lost the war, not the soldiers."

"Your father," Schwarz began, "he must have been quite a soldier during the war. I suppose old habits die hard."

"And old soldiers *never* die," she said, smiling tentatively. "But, yes, my father was quite a fighter. He led the Gray Wolf Brigade back in Vietnam during the war. They were very elusive, very fearless. They were trained by your Green Berets, an American Indian soldier. A full-blooded Cherokee, they say. This Indian…he came up with the name Gray Wolf Brigade. Even after he was killed the following year, the name stuck."

Haley was the only one in the group not taking part in the conversation. She stared at the dancer's turquoise eyes, wondering what ten million dollars in emeralds looked like. They'd let her in on that much about the case: a couple of fast operators had smuggled the jewels out of Vietnam and Lyons's buddies had been hired by the U.S. government to retrieve the stones in hopes of avoiding an international incident. At least *that* was the official line, but Klein wasn't sure she was buying it. They seemed more like a misfit trio, soldiers of *mis*fortune, than any mercenaries for hire. But then she recalled the shoot-out back in San Francisco's Chinatown. Carl Lyons certainly knew his business. She wondered how good his two cohorts were under fire.

It was then that she noticed the black sedan speeding down Moran Street toward the Dragon's Tooth Gift Shop. The perforated black barrel of an Uzi submachine gun was sticking out of the driver's side window.

"We've got trouble!" Klein yelled.

Lyons, Schwarz and Blancanales all turned toward the shop's front windows at her warning. The policewoman had already drawn her pistol.

"This is unbelievable," Haley muttered under her breath as she sought cover just inside the doorway. "When does it end?"

As if backing up his old police partner during a room-to-room search for a felon, Lyons automatically took up a position to the right and rear of her until he could assess the situation. They all heard the increasing roar of a car engine on the street outside as the black sedan approached at high speed.

"Get down!" Blancanales yelled at the cashier. Schwarz rushed toward her, but he was too late.

A burst of rifle slugs exploded through several of the shop's front windows, and a deafening roar of discharges filled the Dragon's Tooth as Lyons and Klein responded with pistol shot after pistol shot.

"Get on the phone!" Haley yelled in Blancanales's direction as she dropped into a defensive crouch, ejected six empty cartridges from her revolver and fumbled with another half-dozen fresh rounds. "Dial 911. Get us some—"

"*We* can handle it!" Politician joined them at the doorway, unloading his modified Colt .45 as the vehicle slid into a sideways skid directly in front of the store. Eight hollowpoints ripped through the driver's side door and window in a tight grouping.

"I know that!" Klein yelled back, fire in her eyes as she rose to her feet, leaned against the door frame, fired two bullets at the car's front tire, then two more at the spinning rear wheel. "But do you want to chase this guy on foot?"

"You're right!" Blancanales said, nodding, although he didn't move toward the phone. Instead, he ejected the automatic's spent clip and slammed a fresh seven-round magazine up into the empty handle. "But I was hoping to stop the scum in their tracks. Right here!"

"Guess again!" Klein said, shaking her head back and forth helplessly as the car fishtailed from side to side and began accelerating back down Moran Street the way it had come. "Now get on that damn phone, or I'll do it myself!" She holstered her .38 as the sedan sped out of range.

"No time for that!" Lyons said, already out the door and sprinting toward a motorcyclist, who had pulled over to the side of the road when the first exchange of shots had begun. "Come on!"

Blancanales holstered his .45 and rushed out the door after Ironman.

"Oh, shit," Gadgets moaned as he dropped to his knees behind the cashier's counter.

"My God, no!" Haley cried, freezing behind him.

A three-round burst of slugs had caught the woman in the face, just below her eyes. From cheek to cheek a bloody gash had been hideously torn by the merciless burst of hot lead. Her eyeballs had ruptured from the triple impact. Her lips and lower jaw hung down against her throat, dangling by shreds of bone and gristle, all but severed.

Another innocent bystander had been mowed down by street evil. Klein dropped to one knee, closed her eyes tightly and sighed in resignation.

The sound of a motorcycle speeding away filled her ears, and Haley raised her head. Her eyes focused on the jagged shards of amber porcelain lying all around the woman's lifeless body. It took a while to realize what she was looking at, and then she spotted the turquoise eyes staring back at her from the pool of blood collecting on the floor.

The shooter's assault had destroyed *two* beautiful women. Several bullets had struck the statue dead center, ripping it apart.

13

Lyons had tried to be polite about it, but when the motorcyclist refused to surrender his Kawasaki 750, Ironman had no other choice: he decked the wiry Vietnamese. "Consider it lawfully commandeered!" he advised the man.

"We'll try to get it back to you in one piece!" Blancanales had added.

Now, Rosario clinging to his waist, the ex-LAPD cop roared eastbound down the busy Bolsa Strip, slowly gaining on the speeding black sedan.

Bolsa was almost always congested with bumper-to-bumper traffic. Today it seemed even worse. The black sedan clipped several slower-moving vehicles as it swerved from lane to lane, trying to get away.

"Think he sees us?" Blancanales yelled into Lyons's ear as their motorcycle raced down the raised lane dividers between two endless lines of cars and trucks.

"Based on the way he's driving, yeah!"

"Can you see his license plate?"

"Appears to be taped over!"

"Just get us up there a little closer, Ironman, and I'll bust some caps through his rear window. That'll get his attention!"

"Where are the local cops when you need 'em most?"

To their left, huge ornamental dragon arches guarding one of the biggest market plazas in Little Saigon rose in majestic tribute to the success of Orange County's newest immigrants. To their right, the impressive Asian Garden Mall, with its three levels of green tile roofing and giant marble Buddha statues out front, further attested to the increasing prosperity of Bolsa's Vietnamese merchants.

"Can you tell what kind of car that is?" Pol yelled.

"Looks like one of those snazzy new Monte Carlos," Ironman said as he gritted his teeth.

"Boy, if that baby makes it to the freeway, we're up shit creek, Ironman! It's got some *bad* pistons under the hood!"

"That's what I've heard!" Lyons said, nodding as he swerved between two delivery trucks, just as both were making illegal lane changes without bothering to signal.

Blancanales ducked as a rear fender clipped the Kawasaki's right mirror. Glass exploded, sending shards across the roadway behind them.

A siren began wailing. Lyons glanced over his shoulder and realized that a Westminster motorcycle cop was attempting to catch up with them. From a side street two black-and-whites also appeared, their lights flashing.

"Good! *Good!*" Blancanales was nodding wildly as he waved the officer up, but as they entered the next intersection against the green signal lights, a souped-up '57 Ford raced through, broadsiding the police motorcycle.

"Shit!" Lyons yelled, feeling a wave of nausea swirl through his gut as he caught a glimpse of the officer being hurled several dozen feet through the air by the impact.

"Should we stop?" Blancanales asked, his grasp around Lyons's belly tight as a vise now.

Ironman didn't answer. Instead, he concentrated on his driving. And accelerating. Out of the corner of one eye he spotted one of the patrol cars swerving to the side of the road to render aid to the fallen motorcycle cop, while the second unit continued the pursuit. "Thank God!" he muttered under his breath.

He didn't even know the motorcycle officer who had been broadsided back there, of course, but he felt a pain in his gut as if the man had been his partner. And he wanted this scumbag in the black Monte Carlo now more than ever!

At the major intersection running north and south through the heart of Little Saigon, everyone slowed to make the left-hand turn but, within seconds, had increased their speed again. The Westminster patrol car was suddenly roaring up on Lyons's left.

The officer riding shotgun leaned out the passenger door, Remington 12-gauge braced in both hands. He planted the barrel next to Ironman's ear. "Pull that bike over right now!" he demanded, spittle flying from between his lips, eyes bulging. "Or your head is history!"

From his own years policing the streets of L.A., Lyons knew how cops thought. He also knew he was about two seconds away from a double-aught buck decapitation. But the tension didn't show on his face. Nor did he slow the Kawasaki. Instead, he shouted back, "Federal agents! Help us get that Monte Carlo!"

Both uniformed patrolmen leaned toward their windshield for a better view of the traffic ahead, as if they'd just noticed the Monte Carlo for the first time, which they probably had. They had obviously been concentrating their efforts on the speeding motorcycle.

The 12-gauge moved from behind Lyons's ear, and Ironman let out a sigh of relief as the black-and-white Caprice lurched ahead, pistons rattling in protest as its driver forced the engine into overdrive, even though it was already traveling at ninety miles per hour. The cop's goal was obvious: overtake the Monte Carlo before it reached the next intersection, ram it while they were still on the relatively empty straightaway that led up to Hazard Street.

"I'm sure glad you're such a fast talker!" Blancanales yelled into Ironman's ear as they kept their heads low, trying to keep up with the Westminster patrol car.

Again Lyons didn't respond—he was too busy concentrating on the traffic up ahead. Although most cars yielded the right-of-way to the police car, they almost immediately swerved back out onto the roadway after it passed, which was a continuous test of Ironman's defensive driving skills. More than once he nearly lost control as sudden swerves sent the Kawasaki down so low that the kickstand gouged asphalt out of the pavement, showering startled motorists on either side of them with sparks. Glass shards from the shattered mirror continued to peel off, embedding themselves in the thighs of both men.

"Aw, shit," Lyons muttered under his breath as the signal light up ahead switched to red and cross traffic began filling the intersection, the drivers oblivious to the danger fast approaching them.

The Monte Carlo driver didn't even slow down, however. Two plumes of black smoke rose from his dual exhausts as he gunned the engine, bursting through heavy traffic with his horn blaring. He almost made it to the other side unscathed, but a Volkswagen Beetle clipped the Monte Carlo's right rear quarter panel.

Spinning like a top, the VW bounced over a raised curb and rolled through the front wall of a Vietnamese café, while the Monte Carlo's rear end slid slightly to the left. The driver quickly brought his vehicle under control again, however, and proceeded northbound on Brookhurst into Restaurant Row.

The Westminster police car wasn't so lucky. Although its driver slowed for the red light, hardly anyone was paying attention to his yelping siren and flashing lights now. They all seemed to be gawking at the overturned VW and the patrons fleeing the demolished restaurant.

A delivery van slammed into the patrol car's right front fender, hurling it to the left into oncoming lanes, where it was then struck by a small airport bus and brought to a dead stop. Two more vehicles left several dozen feet of skid marks before slamming into the patrol car, knocking it over onto its left side.

At a hair under a hundred miles an hour, the Kawasaki was fast approaching a similar fate, for the intersection was now packed with dozens of cars that had spun out, rear-ended, or broadsided one another. Even a skilled motor-cyclist like Ironman would be unable to simply swerve around the catastrophe, for it extended out onto the side-walks and storefronts on both sides and was growing with each passing second as more automobiles slammed into the melee of twisting metal and bouncing tires.

It was all he could do to keep the bike under control. Not many men were able to leave a hundred-foot, two-wheeled skid mark without slamming their bike down at the end of the ride. Lyons was no ordinary man.

When they finally came to a stop, Blancanales's voice had risen an octave or two. "I thought we were dead, Carl!"

The black Monte Carlo was long gone.

A TATTERED SCROLL had fluttered down, unnoticed, from inside the porcelain dancer statue when it had been ripped to pieces by the burst of automatic weapons fire.

As Lyons, Klein and the others stood by now, watching Westminster homicide detectives gather evidence inside the Dragon's Tooth Gift Shop, the rolled-up sheet of cracked and yellowing paper was spotted and retrieved by Ironman, without the investigators' knowledge.

The motorcycle officer broadsided at the intersection of Bolsa and Bushard was dead on arrival at the hospital, where he was airlifted by a flight-for-life helicopter within ten minutes of the crash. He died of massive head and in-ternal injuries, leaving behind a widow and four young sons.

In contrast, the two officers involved in the multiple-car crash at Brookhurst and Hazard Streets received only mi-nor injuries. They were able to walk away from their to-talled patrol car, and even maintained the energy to wrestle down and arrest one of the other drivers involved in the ac-cident—a belligerent and combative drunk who later blew a three-point-five on the breathalyzer, *after* receiving thirty-five stitches at the emergency room for resisting.

None of the Able Team commandos revealed their true role in the escalation of recent events from San Francisco to Orange County. They told investigators that they were merely shopping for souvenirs at the Dragon's Tooth when a madman drove by and sprayed the shop with machine gun fire. Lyons and Blancanales gave chase but, as the other officers could attest to, lost the suspect in heavy traffic.

The owner of the Kawasaki claimed he was going to sue everyone involved, but his tune changed when one of the traffic investigators ran a check on the man and several felony warrants for previous "failures-to-appear" on narcotics charges were found to be outstanding on him. As he was being led away in handcuffs, Blancanales slipped a business card into the man's pocket. "Send us the bill for that damage to the mirror," Pol told the prisoner.

"That won't be necessary," a sergeant said, retrieving the card and returning it to Blancanales without reading it. "For *some* unknown reason," he said sarcastically, locking eyes with the arrestee, "the serial number on his Kawasaki was altered. That means it gets impounded."

"So book me," the Vietnamese man sighed. "Before you guys find something else out about me and my wheels."

Haley slipped up and flashed her SFPD shield when asked for identification, a weakness of most cops when confronted by other members of the Brotherhood of the Badge. The investigator who eyeballed the San Francisco star seemed intrigued, but didn't ask what she was doing in the company of the three hard-core survivalist types.

"Nasty cut over your eye there," the detective said, motioning at the wound Haley had received during the Chrysanthemum Café shoot-out. He seemed to be searching his memory, too. Hadn't he read somewhere about a San Francisco policewoman getting blasted while trying to arrest some Viet thugs in Chinatown? "They got you working cover car up there or something?'' He was referring to the four-man units that patrolled the more violent areas of town during the busy daytime period, responding to bar fights, family disturbances and radio calls for backup. Cops working the cover cars usually taped over their name tags, or removed them entirely, prior to roll call.

"It's a tough job, but—" Haley began.

"Some *woman's* got to do it."

Klein smiled. "There it is," she said. They'd obviously heard of policewomen's civil rights down here in Orange County, too.

Lyons and the rest of Able Team claimed to be free-lance writers when asked about their occupations—Ironman and Politician could only hope they were long gone before the two patrolmen involved in the chase showed up. They had identified themselves as federal agents to the cops.

"So, do you have any idea what the motive for this senseless act of violence may have been?" Lyons asked one of the detectives.

All of the detectives turned to stare at Lyons. His choice of words marked him as a cop or a reporter. Perhaps both. "Gangs, probably," one of the detectives finally responded.

"Were they receiving threats here at the Dragon's Tooth? Extortion-type threats?" Ironman asked, staring at the blanket covering the young woman's lifeless body.

"All these little mom-and-pop stores get hit up by the gang-bangers, friend," a detective said. "It's a fact of life here in Little Saigon, just one of the extra costs of doing business along Bolsa."

"But nothing specific?"

The investigator's eyes narrowed again. "Specific?"

"I mean, you're not looking at any specific gang or suspect for this particular murder? No political angle?"

The detective's features softened. If he was momentarily suspicious of Lyons's line of questioning, his expression also told the ex-cop that he was overworked and didn't get paid enough to read innuendo into some half-cocked witness's cryptic choice of words. "Oh, you mean about the victim here being the General's daughter?"

"How do you think this General guy's gonna react to his baby girl getting wasted?" Blancanales asked.

"Well, we haven't seen Old Man Pham around town the past couple of weeks. He's probably raisin' hell over in Thailand or some such place, terrorizing the customs officials and border guards over there, trying to sneak across the border into Vietnam via Laos. But I'm sure that once word gets to him, all hell's gonna break loose. You can bank on that prediction."

"If we don't find out who blew her away," one of the other investigators said, chuckling, "Old Man Pham definitely will. We'll probably end up bustin' his ass for the mass-murder of some entire gook gang over in Santa Ana or Garden Grove."

"What about this freedom fighter shit?" Lyons asked. "Is there really a bona fide resistance movement still going on back in Nam? I heard those poor guys got wiped out back in '81 or '82."

"There are five or six different factions fighting for control of the jungle surrounding Saigon," the senior detective said. Lyons recognized him, from one of Brognola's intelligence briefs, as the area's Asian gang expert. "Pham supposedly heads a group called Tu Do Luc Quan. They're bigtime. CIA supposedly arms them with automatic weapons and a bunch of high-tech night-fighting equipment. But it's only a matter of time...."

"Only a matter of time?" Schwarz asked.

"Until Tu Do Luc Quan gets wiped off the Indochinese map, too. The People's Army of Vietnam has just gotten too strong since 1975, gentlemen. Shit, we left half our MACV and USARV arsenals over there for the South Vietnamese, you know. And what did ARVN go and do? Turn tail and run, man. Left all that crap behind for Charlie to scoop up without so much as a fight. If these people really think some ragtag outfit of freedom fighters is ever going to liberate their homeland, they're just fantasizing a bad dream, believe me.''

"Shit,'' the other detective said, laughing. "You think these people really want to go back to Nam?'' He laughed harder the second time. "It took me five years working Orange County's Little Saigon beat to remember something I learned my first day on the street as an MP in Saigon. It's the dream of every Vietnamese to get to America, by hook or by crook. Therefore, I find it hard as hell to believe these 'new immigrants' harbor any desire to return to Vietnam, even to liberate their homeland. It's all money-oriented. All that bullshit about ancestor worship and needing to return to the soil of their birth is nothing but hogwash, I guarantee you.''

Maybe you should request a transfer to the New Seoul beat, Blancanales was thinking. You might not enjoy working the Bolsa Strip, but the people of Little Saigon certainly don't deserve someone so in need of an attitude adjustment. But Rosario kept silent. They all did. After all, this wasn't home turf. It was Southern California. Never-never land.

"Actually,'' Lyons finally said, "the reason we came down here was to try to get an interview with the General, but nobody seems to know where he lives. I don't suppose *you'd* be privy to information like that, would you?''

"Information 'like that' would be classified,'' the senior detective replied with a frown. "People like Pham try to keep a low profile, which we encourage.''

"I'm sure you wouldn't mind sharing such classified information with a fellow peace officer,'' Haley said, cocking an injured eyebrow at him, the gesture forcing her to wince from the resulting bolt of pain.

The senior detective's frown deepened, but Haley's pained expression elicited a rare show of compassion from the grizzled street veteran. "Well, none of us actually knows where General Pham hangs his helmet. But he seems to show up now and then at the Pho '90 Restaurant. You might check there."

"On Bolsa?" Lyons asked.

"Ten thousand five hundred block," the senior detective said, his frown returning. "Or thereabouts."

"We appreciate it," Blancanales said.

"I'm sure you do," the senior detective said. "And *we'd* appreciate it if the four of you would steer clear of any future trouble here in Little Saigon."

"We'll do our best," Lyons promised, turning and leading the others from the cordoned-off crime scene.

"Free-lance writers, my ass," the senior investigator said, chuckling under his breath as Able Team plus Klein exited through the bullet-riddled doorway.

14

"Well, what will it be?" Lyons asked his jaded companions as they settled around a table in an open-air café. "Caffeine or sedatives?"

"I still can't believe how..." Gadgets said, his voice trailing off, only to come back stronger than ever as he relived the shooting again and again in his head. "One moment she was standing there and the next she was dead and so savagely mutilated." He locked eyes with Pol.

Blancanales shook his head slowly in emotional surrender. "I thought I left that kind of ugliness behind in Vietnam. These poor people...they just can't seem to escape all the shit that—"

"*We* brought that shit down on her," Lyons reminded him matter-of-factly.

"How do you mean?"

"That Monte Carlo was the same black sedan that was parked on the highway overlooking the Clifftop Hotel," he answered, staring straight through the ex-Black Beret. "Back in Ventura. You know it and I know it."

"But—"

"No buts, Pol. We should have taken him out of the picture back in Ventura, then and there, whoever the bastard was. Instead, we slacked off, and now that poor kid in there—" he motioned in the direction of the Dragon's Tooth Gift Shop with his chin "—paid the supreme sacrifice without even knowing what the game was all about. Now that sucks, pal, pure and simple.''

"And we still have absolutely no idea who the hell was inside the Monte Carlo,'' Haley said. "Unless there's something *else* you guys aren't telling me.''

"You know everything we know,'' Lyons said quickly. "Take your best shot.''

"I'm still not sure what I have to choose from,'' she said, her words soaked with sarcasm.

"Look, we haven't much to go on at this point,'' Lyons replied, "but I *do* know one thing. That detective across the street back there just gave me an address that matches the one in Tran Van Thieu's journal.''

"The one marked *dai khai*—for the General,'' Haley said.

"Right-O,'' Lyons said with mild satisfaction.

"I'd completely forgotten about that.''

"And I think we'd best have a talk with this General Pham.''

"Maybe if we are the ones to break the death of his daughter to him, Pham will cooperate,'' Blancanales said.

Lyons's grin warped into an irritated frown, though he wasn't upset with Politician. "I can just about guarantee you that Little Saigon's wait-a-minute vine gets word of the girl's murder to the General long before we're ever able to track him down.''

"Wait-a-minute vine?'' Haley said, appearing perplexed.

"The Bolsa grapevine,'' Gadgets explained. "Rumor Control.''

"Oh...''

"The best we can hope for,'' Lyons went on, "is to intercept Pham before he heads out on the warpath. If we don't get to him before then, he might go underground for weeks...*months*, even. And if he goes crazy over his daughter's death, he might end up behind bars before we get a chance to talk to him.''

"Set me straight on one thing," Gadgets requested as they all continued to stare down at their menus without developing an appetite. "Just exactly what information is this General Pham going to provide us with, assuming we locate him in time, and assuming he cooperates?"

"Good question," Lyons said, his grin tired.

"What?"

He showed Gadgets and Politician Tran Van Thieu's diary for the first time. "We went to this guy's address first," he said, running a fingertip under Tran's initials, "and found a woman's nude body."

"Minus her head," Haley added.

"Right," Lyons said. "Now the scroll we found hidden in the subway tunnel lists an address in Little Saigon that turns out to be the Dragon's Tooth Gift Shop."

"And just happens to be managed by General Pham's daughter," Schwarz said. "Hark, a connection."

"Give the man a cigar," Lyons said, pulling a Honduran cigar from an inner pocket of his jacket.

Gadgets didn't smoke, but he was feeling defiant and self-destructive, so he lit up, took a deep puff and began coughing almost immediately. He set the cigar down on the edge of an ashtray.

"So much for the tough man of the year contest," Politician quipped.

"Kiss my—" Schwarz started to say, only to start coughing again. Haley slapped him on the back.

"And now we make another unexpected discovery," Lyons said, removing the second carefully concealed scroll from his pocket and unrolling it for all to see.

"Fourteen addresses again," Haley observed.

"Hey, wait a minute!" Gadgets exclaimed. "They're the same!"

"Yes," Lyons said, nodding solemnly. "They're the same. All fourteen." He produced the scroll found in San

Francisco's Chinatown and laid it beside the one that had been hidden in the Dragon's Tooth statue.

"But what about the Monte Carlo?" Blancanales asked, rubbing his throbbing temples. "Who the hell was driving that damn thing, Ironman? Any ideas? Any at all?"

"There's basically only three possibilities," Lyons said, massaging his eyelids, evidence they were all sorely in need of some much-deserved rest. "Four, if you include the General and his people."

"Give me the first three and we'll go on from there," Blancanales said.

"Okay, number one: the kidnappers of One-eyed Ngoc, although we've got zero clues as to their identity thus far. Number two: the Phi-Chau, an up-and-coming Vietnamese gang gaining ground in San Francisco's Chinatown."

"They'd be my bet," Gadgets opined.

"Number three: the Vietnamese Secret Police."

"Who might actually be your number one suspects, as well," Haley volunteered. "Assuming they're the ones behind One-eyed Ngoc's disappearance."

"The Vietnamese Secret Police?" Blancanales said. "This is getting damn complicated."

"Hey, I don't write the story, Rosario. I just try to tie up all the loose ends with a dynamite climax, okay?"

The desired effect—a round of laughter—wasn't achieved. The others seated around him remained silent, staring down into their cups of mint tea.

"But what about—" A thought had struck Schwarz, and he started to verbalize it when Blancanales suddenly began slapping the table near Gadgets's elbow.

"Hey!" Pol yelled as he grabbed a glass of ice water and threw it on one of the scrolls just as it burst into flames, ignited by the huge, smoldering cigar Gadgets had left unattended.

"Shit!" Schwarz exclaimed, glancing over at Ironman as he helped Blancanales save the scroll from further damage. But it had all but been consumed by the flames.

"Talk about a flash fire!" Haley said, laughing softly as the exhaustion they were all feeling began to take its toll.

"Wait a minute," Gadgets said after lifting the scorched slivers of paper and holding them up to the light of an orange Chinese dragon lantern suspended over their table. "Check this out."

As if by magic, several numbers appeared along one edge of the damaged scroll. "Heat-generated," Lyons told the group as he glanced around to make sure none of the other café patrons were watching.

"What?" Haley asked, leaning closer.

"Someone," Lyons explained, "scribbled these numbers across the scroll, using invisible ink. The paper was then treated chemically, so that when subjected to heat, chemical compounds inside the ink would cause it to reappear."

"Hell, we used to do that kind of crap when we were kids," Blancanales said, seemingly unimpressed. "With milk, I think it was."

"Same principle," Lyons said, nodding. "Different formula. Slightly more sophisticated. But I thought this sort of thing went out of style among espionage types way back in the fifties."

"Around the time the French left Vietnam in disgrace?" Schwarz asked, locking eyes with Ironman, who fell silent at the implications.

There were thirty-five numbers in all. They were laid out one after another in no apparent order, no special configuration.

Lyons was sure that each and every number or sequence of numbers stood for something. Something critical. He wondered if they would finally lead Able Team to the secret documents or the fortune in hidden emeralds. He also wondered how they'd crack the code.

"So what's next?" Gadgets asked innocently, totally befuddled. "Do we travel to the next address on the list? Or what?"

"Well, there's a slight problem here," Ironman announced, staring long and hard at the thirty-five numbers, and the fourteen addresses.

"What?" Haley asked, yawning.

"I've already verified it with an atlas over at the hotel, and there's no doubt."

"No doubt about what?" they all demanded, patience wearing thin.

"None of the other twelve cities on this so-called List of Fourteen even exist."

THE PHO '90 RESTAURANT was a cavernous room with a high ceiling and space for nearly a hundred small tables. The ceiling was high because the structure had once been a warehouse. It was now brightly lit—Oriental lanterns hung below slowly twirling fans suspended from the ceiling every dozen feet or so. The restaurant was so bright, in fact, that young couples looking for more romantic surroundings usually went elsewhere. Most Vietnamese dined for good food, not atmosphere. They went to a restaurant or café because of its reputation. They enjoyed the brightness, wanted to see what they were being served, and were suspicious of dark decor and subdued lighting.

Pho '90 wasn't Spartan or ugly. The owner's son fancied himself an artist, and all the walls had been turned into delightful murals depicting street scenes from Old Saigon. Along one wall: Tu Do. The next: Nguyen Hue. There was a wall dedicated to the maze of back-alley vendor stalls leading to the central market. And the last depicted Saigon by night, with the Rex Cinema's water fountains illuminated by hot pink, purple and red streams of neon. For this reason Pho '90 was often crowded. The murals were the latest thing to come to Little Saigon.

Even this afternoon, at roughly two o'clock, the place was packed to capacity. There was a long line of people waiting for tables. A waiter spotted them entering through the statue-cluttered foyer and waved them up to the front of the line. Chin high, Lyons led the way.

"Carl," Schwarz said, sounding embarrassed at what appeared to be preferential treatment for the only white patrons present.

"Forget it," Ironman replied. "The dude's leading us to that small table against the wall there. Everyone else here is with a larger party and has to wait for two or more tables to clear so they can join them together."

"And this is your *first* time here?" Blancanales asked skeptically.

"Little Saigon, Chinatown," he said flippantly, "it's the same everywhere, amigo."

"Not in Mexico."

"Everywhere that counts."

"Touché!"

After they were seated, Lyons passed a fifty-dollar bill to the waitress who brought them tea. "General Pham," he asked, "has he been in yet today?"

The woman didn't immediately accept the money. "Who?" she asked as she backed away a pace.

"Pham," Schwarz repeated, leaning across the table toward her. "He's with the Resistance."

"The freedom fighters in Vietnam," Blancanales added. His voice wasn't as subtle, and a few heads at the nearest table turned in their direction. "We know he uses Pho '90 as his contact point stateside. In fact, we have it on good authority."

"I'm afraid you gentlemen must be mistaken," she said, batting her long eyelashes gracefully as she began to back away. "I will have one of the waiters bring your menus. Does anyone want cocktails?"

"Ever hear of the Gray Wolves?" Schwarz asked, unsure why the question left his own lips. "The Gray Wolf Brigade?"

"How about Tu Do Luc Quan?" Blancanales added.

"No...I'm sorry." Her eyes narrowed as she turned to leave.

After she was gone, Lyons glanced at the others. "This isn't going to be as easy as I thought it would. Pham obviously keeps a low profile. And these people are tight-lipped."

"We probably look like four FBI agents," Haley said as she tested her tea. The resulting expression was one of mild approval.

"Or four IRS agents," Lyons said, grinning.

They didn't have long to make jokes. Or to order their meals.

The moment their menus were delivered a grating roar caught Ironman's attention. Through the front plate-glass window he saw a white van speed toward the entrance and then crash through the foyer.

"Everybody down!" he yelled. But Lyons wasn't in the company of green recruits. They were already waiting in low crouches, squats or down on one knee, handguns drawn.

The van plowed through four tables filled with diners, overturned onto a fifth and exploded. A dozen people were killed instantly as the C-4 satchel wired to the undercarriage sent shrapnel in the form of nails and shredded barbed wire through the van's walls and through flesh.

Screaming wildly, people fled in all directions. Haley Klein and Able Team started cautiously toward the smoldering van.

"Get the guy in the van!" Schwarz directed. "We've got to get to the driver, if there's anything left of him."

"There won't be," Lyons told them as they advanced through the area of destruction.

"What?" Schwarz questioned.

"I got a glimpse of the van as it was racing up to the entrance. There was nobody in the front seat."

"He's right!" Blancanales confirmed. He had advanced on the vehicle, gun arm extended, ready for a firefight. Lowering his weapon and opening the door, he pointed at the sliver of board braced between the front seat and gas pedal.

Automatically they turned to stare out the restaurant's front windows, which were nothing more than jagged shards now. But if they were hoping the culprits would be waiting down the block, watching the results of their handiwork, Lyons and crew were disappointed. The street outside was now crowded with people rushing over from the nearby malls and shopping plazas to see what had happened.

"Death to all Communists!" one man yelled. He was standing in the middle of all the carnage, holding the lifeless body of his wife in his arms. His clothes were shredded, his face and hands streaked with blood. Her dress was all but gone, torn away by the explosion. What remained of her body was singed and blackened. "I will kill ten of Hanoi's people for every patriot murdered here today!" he vowed, clenched fist raised over his wife's lifeless body. "On the honor of my dead parents, I promise it!"

Haley wasn't convinced the man was correct. "Do you really think the Communists were behind this?" she asked Lyons.

"I wish I could say they were," Ironman answered as he examined a crude warning scrawled in black paint across the van's rear doors. "But *this* seems to contradict that possibility." The sign read:

No place that harbors the killers of our brothers is safe from the vengeance of the Phi-Chau boys! Remember the Chrysanthemum Café massacre.

"You mean this car, this *van* bombing was directed at us?" Schwarz and Blancanales asked incredulously.

"At *us*," Lyons corrected, motioning to Haley, then himself.

"Those Chinatown gang-bangers followed us all the way down here from San Francisco?" Klein questioned, glancing around, scanning the dazed, bloodied faces for hostile eyes.

"It would seem so," Ironman said. "Or else they had connections here in Little Saigon and notified them to hit us at the first opportunity."

"But 'harbors'?" Anger flashed in Haley's green eyes. "This restaurant wasn't harboring us, or anyone else. We just stopped in here for something to eat."

"And to touch base with Pham," Blancanales reminded her.

"Typical gang tactic," Lyons said. "Terrorize as many people as possible while going after your primary target of opportunity, regardless of any connection between your prey and the general populace. Let's get out of here," Lyons continued as a growing crescendo of sirens in the distance reached their ears. "I tend to believe our welcome with the local law-enforcement community will have grown mighty thin if they find us in the middle of another... incident."

"Speaking as a cop," Haley said, "I tend to agree with you."

MAJOR TRUONG SLOWLY LOWERED his American-made M-700 sniper rifle. He carefully replaced the telescopic scope's lens cap and slipped the heavy weapon into the customized golf bag he had been using to ferry it around from job to job. What had transpired in front of his cross hairs as he was about to shoot Carl Lyons between the eyes had been completely unexpected—a van had crashed through the front wall of the restaurant! A van delivered by some overzealous young gangsters with a naive dedication and out-of-date ideology.

The bombing had interrupted Truong's planned assassination of General Pham, but there had been no real guarantee that the Resistance leader would even show up at Pho '90 today—he hadn't been seen in public in weeks. So Truong—convinced he would never be able to retrieve Tran Van Thieu's diary from Lyons and his comrades while they were still alive—had opted for taking as many of the nosy Americans out of the picture as he could.

Truong was convinced of this because he'd just received a coded teletype from the Vietnamese Association in New York. He wasn't dealing with some misfit bunch of mercenaries out to make a fast buck as amateur detectives. He'd locked horns with the U.S. government's covert Able Team. Now his immediate objectives had changed drastically: forget the documents, forget the emeralds. The General could wait. Terminate Lyons, Schwarz, Blancanales and the San Francisco policewoman. *That* had become the primary objective for Major Truong.

Until the van crashed into his plans. Now the situation had unexpectedly changed again. And Truong was struck by an idea. It seemed he and these crazy Phi-Chau boys had the same long-range goals in mind.

Perhaps Truong and the Phi-Chau could form some sort of arrangement that would prove beneficial to both their groups. The prospect made Truong chuckle. An arrangement that would prove mutually beneficial to both their groups....

15

With the headlights of his black Monte Carlo off, Major Truong coasted up to the edge of L.A. Pier 68, less than a mile from the deep-water port. It was a few minutes before midnight; nearly nine hours had passed since the terrorist bombing at Pho '90. The Bolsa Strip was still sealed off in both directions for several blocks. He was glad to get out of Orange County for a while—the police down there were stopping every grim-faced Asian who looked out of place, and a man with Truong's experienced countenance behind the wheel of a black Monte Carlo *would* have alerted any street cop worth his salt.

Truong let himself relax somewhat, although he never let down his guard entirely. He knew he had enemies everywhere.

He glanced to his left and to his right. He checked over both shoulders before getting out of the car, but he was definitely alone. No one was working late at this particular loading dock. There was only one old freighter tied up on the other side of the pier, several hundred feet away. No one had followed him. He had made sure of that. Truong was schooled in evasive driving maneuvers, and in avoiding the situations that would require evasive driving maneuvers in the first place. Tonight he would have spotted even Able Team.

He left the car's engine running as he got out of the vehicle and limped around to the back, cursing the leg wound he'd received in San Francisco. It was tightly wrapped with bandages now, and healing slowly, stiffly.

Truong opened the trunk and stared down at the sweat-soaked human cowering before him. Bound and gagged, a trembling Ngoc Ung Mau stared up at him, terror in his one remaining eye.

Without showing any emotion, Truong drew a small .38 Smith & Wesson pistol from inside his gray sport jacket and slowly attached a sophisticated silencer to the end of the barrel. "I'm going to kill you with your own gun, Ngoc—the ultimate insult to a soldier."

A sick, demented chuckle followed this announcement. "Yes, in the good old days you were a great soldier, Ngoc. But with old age came selfishness on your part—selfishness and greed. You forgot about the Cause. You betrayed the Party."

Ngoc struggled to say something, but the tape wrapped across his mouth and tightly around the back of his head prevented him. For a moment, as he bent slightly, it appeared Truong might rip away the gag and allow Ngoc some last words. But this wouldn't be the case tonight. Truong just threw his head back and let out a hideous, almost demonic laugh.

"It has come to my attention that your friend Tran has also betrayed the Party, that he has gone over to the American side." Truong paused as Ngoc's eyes seemed to bulge with muted protest. "Oh, I know what you want to say. You want to stick up for your old friend Tran. You want to claim he was kidnapped by the Americans, that they *made* him talk, eh? Well, we know better, Ngoc, old friend. Tran turned, and you were about to turn, only we found out in time. Fool! Recovering the prize no longer means so much to me. The emeralds are even less important, if they even exist.

"What's that odd twist to your features, Ngoc, old friend?" Truong seemed to detect a sudden calmness flooding his prisoner's face, a certain relief. "Oh, about the prize? The President's prize? Yes, I knew. The others don't. They still think I'm out in the field trying to track down some documents, but we know better, don't we, Ngoc? You and Mot Bo Bay—your childish Cult Of Seven—began with a little unexpected loot. Ten million U.S. dollars' worth of emeralds to be exact. And you ended up having to hide the piece of Vietnamese national treasure unlawfully removed from Hanoi by Tran—an article worth ten times as much as your damn emeralds, a hundred times as much!

"Well, enough talk, my old friend. My partner, Major Chen Chi Vinh, sacrificed his life recently, trying to help me accomplish my mission. And for his death someone must also pay the supreme sacrifice. That someone is you, Ngoc. Yes, you forgot about the Cause. You betrayed the Party. And now your time is up." He raised the gun until the elongated silencer was pointing at an angle into the car trunk.

Calmly, deliberately, Truong shot Ngoc in the forehead. Once, twice, three times, until the cranium had split open down the middle and there was no doubt the man was dead. Then Truong slowly unscrewed the silencer and pocketed the piece. He carefully wiped his fingerprints off the revolver, dropped it into the trunk on top of Ngoc and slammed the trunk shut. The secret police major then walked off into the nearby shadows and took several minutes to observe his surroundings, but it didn't appear that anyone had noticed the murder.

He walked back out to the Monte Carlo, reached in through the driver's window and turned the ignition key. After the engine rumbled to life, he pulled the gearshift down into Drive and allowed the car to coast off under its own, slowly increasing speed. At the edge of the wharf the Monte Carlo crashed through a wooden barrier and dropped thirty or forty feet into the water. Bubbling viciously in protest, it took only three or four minutes to sink.

Truong didn't know exactly how deep it was here, but a dockhand had assured him it was at least three hundred feet. That should be deep enough.

After junking the Monte Carlo, Truong returned to the shadows and waited ten more minutes—just to be sure— then calmly began walking toward the next pier, several hundred yards and a dozen commercial docks up the sea lane. The major took his time. There was no hurry.

At L.A. Pier 74 he spotted a baby-blue security van with Twenty-four Hour Armed Response emblazoned across its sides. It was parked beside a sagging barbed wire fence. Keeping to the middle of the roadway, and in full view of the guard shack rising behind the van, he continued toward the vehicle until he was bathed in the brilliant silver beam of a stationary floodlight protruding from the ground.

The guard shack was very small and not equipped with a fan or even mosquito wire, so most of the guards chose to spend their shift sitting outside beside a length of slowly burning rope. The lingering smoke kept most of the bugs away. The guards propped their feet on a picnic table while they read or wrote a letter or slept. Tonight the guard was watching a baseball game on his small battery-powered TV. He glanced up upon noticing Truong's approach, but wasn't particularly alarmed by the intruder. After all, this wasn't West Germany or Checkpoint Charlie; it was the ninth inning and the Dodgers were behind by one. And the limping visitor was wearing a three-piece suit. How much of a threat could he be? And what was there worth stealing at this half-empty container dock, anyway?

His eyes returned to the screen and he resumed munching on a bacon-and-egg sandwich. But the guard's eyes were quickly drawn from the sudden bases-loaded home run even before the ball was out of the park. Before he could remove the sandwich from his mouth and reach for his pistol, the Vietnamese man had walked right up to him.

Suddenly producing a Victory MC-5 automatic in .41 Action Express mode, Truong shot the guard in the middle of the forehead, point-blank. There was no struggle, no reaction at all. A half-eaten sandwich tumbled to the ground and broke apart.

Using his foot, Truong pushed the body—still propped up grotesquely in its folding metal chair—over backward into a clump of tall weeds beside the picnic table. Truong then stole the dead guard's portable television set and his baby-blue security van.

It took Gadgets Schwarz a good minute and a half to feed the complicated series of codes and counter codes through both the phone lines and his lap-top computer, finally linking up with the Bear's Lair, back in Virginia.

Aaron Kurtzman was the terror of Stony Man Farm. Paralyzed from the waist down during a siege that had occurred on the grounds several years back, he began every morning with stretch exercises and a strict weight training regimen, designed to strengthen his upper body. Now Kurtzman was the group's computer genius—surpassing even Gadgets's expertise.

"No, it's nothing like that," Schwarz was saying into the phone with a grin. "No, no, not that, either. Just a bunch of numbers, Bear—thirty-five of them to be exact. Now prepare to copy." Schwarz read off the numbers they had discovered on the burned scroll: 24033206508100101778063208399223040.

"You've got to be kidding," Kurtzman responded.

"Negative," Schwarz said, his tone turning serious. He made Kurtzman repeat the numbers to him. "Okay, you've got them down in the right sequence. Now I want you to run them through every Military Intelligence computer bank you can possibly access within the next twenty-four hours and get back to me quicker than ASAP."

"Twenty-four hours?" Bear responded sarcastically. "You're giving me a *whole* twenty-four hours?"

"That's why you get to drive that fancy electric wheelchair all over town," Schwarz quipped.

"You do realize, of course, that it's four in the morning here?"

"And one in the morning here," Schwarz countered.

"Which means I should get at least twenty-seven hours to work on this."

"The chief of the FBI might need twenty-seven hours," Gadgets challenged. "Ironman and Politician seemed to think you could hack it in half the time."

The line went dead without a retort.

"So what do we do now?" Haley asked as she studied the scroll once again.

"Two of you can go out and catch a movie or something," Lyons said as he carefully peeked out through the blinds of their second-floor hotel room at the Lion's Head Inn. Not much activity out in the street, he noted. A police car or two on routine patrol. Behind the hotel a blue security van sat parked and unattended. It was there to offer a false sense of security to the hotel patrons, he assumed.

"At one in the morning there aren't many movie houses open," Schwarz replied, glancing at the wall clock, an amber-colored plastic module in the shape of Vietnam with three red slashes across the center.

"Yeah, I guess you're right," Lyons said, shrugging as he yawned. "Sorry about that. Life's tough, and then you—"

"But how about midnight chow?" Blancanales suggested. "Me and *Officer* Klein will go first, eh, Haley?" He batted his dark eyes at her. "I'm sure we can roust some old mama-san to fry up some eggs or something."

"It would be a pleasure," Klein replied as she stood up.

"Fine," Schwarz said, nodding. "You two head out first. Take your time. Chow down, check out the lobby. Who

knows? This is a Viet hotel. Maybe they've got all-night
kung fu movies on the VCR downstairs."

"Far out," Klein said without enthusiasm. "Too cool."

"We'll be expecting your relief by sunrise," Lyons reminded them.

"And no hanky-panky," Gadgets added. He didn't notice that he was the only one who laughed at the remark, for
his eyes were glued to data racing across the screen of his
portable computer.

KURTZMAN PHONED BACK in less than four hours. "Thirty-
five numbers, eh?" were his first words.

"That's all we gave you to work with. Sorry."

"Well, it's not a phone number—local, national *or* international. Simply not divisible. And it's nobody's social security number or military service number—again not
divisible."

"What about one of the old military service numbers, the
ones used before we went to the nine-digit format?"

"Possible but not probable. The computer hasn't kicked
anything back, anyway. I'm also running it through NATO,
querying allied nation armed forces, just in case."

"What are the odds of checking to see if it's PAVN?"

Bear didn't hesitate. "People's Army of Vietnam?"

"The same."

"I'll give it a whirl, but no promises. I'll phone a few
bigwigs at the Pentagon—intelligence types. Find out what
the NVA used during the war. See if there's a possibility
there."

"They probably haven't changed their procedures much."

"Right. But, Gadgets, I *did* get two possible kickbacks on
this number of yours."

"You did?" Schwarz exploded. "Why didn't you say
so?"

"Because they're long shots and—"

"Let's have it!" Schwarz commanded, plopping open a pocket notebook and punching the button on his pen.

"Well, your thirty-five-digit number *is* divisible into zips."

"What?"

"It breaks down into seven American zip codes."

"*Postal* zip codes?"

"Right. But only *if* you reverse the numbers."

"Aw, shit!"

"Yeah, I know. Not exactly what you were hoping for. But here's the other thing: the number also corresponds with a serial number in the Department of the Interior's list of zoo animals."

"So?"

"Wolves."

A long sigh escaped Schwarz. "Let's have it. We've absolutely nothing else to go on right now. Out with it."

"*Canis lupus.*"

"*Canis* what?"

"*Canis lupus,*" Kurtzman repeated. "Gray wolf. The Denver Zoo's got one. That's what the number came back to: *Canis Lupus*, City Zoo, Denver, Colorado. Actually, they've got four of the predators in residence there. Does it ring a bell at all—gray wolf? I mean, could it be related in any way?"

My father was quite a fighter. He led the Gray Wolf Brigade back in Vietnam during the war.... The words of General Pham's daughter returned to haunt him. *They were very elusive, very fearless—trained by your Green Berets, an American Indian soldier. A full-blooded Cherokee, they say. This Indian ... he came up with the name Gray Wolf Brigade. Even after he was killed the following year, the name stuck....* "Yeah, Aaron," Gadgets said. "It rings a bell. Now how about giving me those zip codes you were talking about."

After he'd written them down on his notepad, Gadgets stared at the seven cities for a moment:

Freeport, Maine
Hilton Head, South Carolina
Plymouth, Massachusetts
Angel Fire, New Mexico
Greenwich Village, New York
Montpelier, Vermont
Little Torch Key, Florida

None of the names meant anything to him, nor did they seem to tie into anything involving the case—either in Little Saigon or Chinatown. He handed the list to Ironman, who shook his head. None of the cities or states registered.

"What about Numbnuts? You guys been able to break him yet?" Schwarz asked Kurtzman. Numbnuts was the code name for Tran Van Thieu.

"He's a tough cookie to crack," Bear replied. "The Chief's still working on him but, as of right now, you're to proceed on this thing as if Numbnuts was dead, as if we'll never get anything out of him."

"In other words, it's unlikely he'll spill any good clues near the end of this caper."

"Affirmative," Bear replied.

"What about those zip codes?"

"Right now they're my second option. Which means I'm going to try not to think about them. They're seven big question marks—that's what they are. And spread out too far."

"Right. What about the General?"

"You're just *full* of interesting questions early in the morning, aren't you?"

"It's my job. And yours is to report. Unless you'd like to speak directly to the Chief."

"Funny man," Schwarz said before he cleared his throat. "Okay, as far as the General goes, he's been a no-show ever since our arrival in Little Saigon. A woman we believe to be his daughter was killed yesterday, however."

"*What?*" Kurtzman demanded.

Schwarz filled him in briefly about Pham's daughter and the shoot-out at Bolsa's Dragon's Tooth Gift Shop. "Nothing's confirmed yet, though. I wanted to touch base with Pham before I filed my report with Stony Man Farm. But—" he scanned his notes and the scribbled reference to gray wolves at the Denver Zoo "—the General will just have to wait. We'll have to take a private flight to Denver, but, Bear, have that wise guy flyboy Jack Grimaldi meet us at Stapleton International with the Lear Jet. I have a feeling we're going to need some private wings to ferry us about the country before this whole thing is over."

"He'll be waiting for you in Denver."

16

In the basement boiler room beneath the Lion's Head Inn on Bolsa Avenue, Major Truong squatted in front of the circuit board of the hotel's telephone switching system. Wires ran from the phone bank to a portable computer sitting on his lap and to headphones covering his ears.

Truong typed feverishly as he listened to the conversation between Gadgets Schwarz and Aaron "the Bear" Kurtzman. He typed the information about the wolves at the Denver Zoo, and he typed in the seven zip codes with their corresponding cities—the whole time frowning, the whole time thinking back to his raid on Ngoc's Chinatown apartment. He wondered if all this information had been hidden somewhere in the seventh-floor flat, and how the hell had he and Chen missed it? And how much time could he have saved if only they'd found it then? If Ngoc had talked, perhaps his partner Captain Chen would still be alive.

But, no, Ngoc had been too greedy. Ngoc had held out to the bitter end, for the ten million in emeralds—or the promise of them—was all Ngoc had left in the world.

Ten million in emeralds...

At Truong's side, a cassette whirred noiselessly, making a permanent record of the phone conversation he was monitoring. Suddenly the motor began to groan in protest with each rotation of the tape wheels! Were the batteries dying, he wondered.

And then Truong remembered that the tape recorder wasn't battery-operated at all, but powered by an electric cord he'd plugged into a nearby voltage outlet. His eyes scanned the dimly lit basement cubicle.

A light over the fuse box fluctuated with power surges. That must be it: the building was prone to power surges! Damn the American way of building things—and the Vietnamese habit of overburdening the system. Truong would be so glad to be done with this mission and be back in New York City, awaiting a Concorde flight to Paris. Ah, France...

He was rapidly tiring of the game being played between Washington and Hanoi. The Americans could have the damn Presidential Prize, for all Truong cared—if indeed it existed. And he wasn't entirely convinced that it did. The emeralds? Perhaps. Documents of some sort? Most certainly. But this priceless treasure his senior contact had taken to calling the Presidential Prize? Truong scoffed at the idea. Not at all possible! Not even if Buddha himself were to walk right into the room and tell him it was so.

At least he didn't *think* it was possible.

Truong listened as Schwarz and Kurtzman completed their conversation and then, after they both hung up their phones, he began disassembling the tap with a nervous swiftness to his actions.

Denver! He certainly didn't want to follow anyone to Denver, Colorado. Truong had been there before.

As ABLE TEAM WAS PREPARING to leave their room at Little Saigon's Lion's Head Inn, the phone rang. The four comrades hesitated in the doorway, staring back at the red blinking light atop the receiver. It was a half hour before sunrise. Who could possible be calling them at predawn?

"Get it," Lyons told Schwarz, who picked up the receiver without saying anything.

"Gadgets? Is that you?"

"What is it?" Schwarz asked, detecting the sudden note of concern in Kurtzman's tone. It flooded his own now.

"Just thought you guys should know about something suspicious. I detected it during a routine equipment scan after you broke off our last telephone communication."

"Something suspicious?"

"Yeah. An electromagnetic feedback surge in the—"

"Feedback surge?"

"Right. That means just one possibility."

"Don't tell me," Schwarz said, thinking about everything they'd discussed: General Pham, his daughter, *Canis lupus* and the Denver Zoo, Numbnuts, the zip codes.

"Someone either tapped your line or ours—and you know this place. I don't think it could have happened on this end."

"Thanks. We'll take care of it."

"If it's not too late."

"Right."

Schwarz hung up the phone and stared silently at Lyons.

"What is it?" Haley asked.

"Around here," Blancanales began, "when Hermann gets that twinkle in his eye, we don't ask that question."

"Trouble," Gadgets said, nodding for the record.

MAJOR TRUONG PROCEEDED to a phone booth located beside an all-night convenience store at the other end of the Bolsa Strip. Shielding his face from the rising sun, he dialed a long-distance number with a San Francisco area code.

It took nearly a dozen rings for someone on the other end to answer. "No one home," a slurred, sleepy voice groaned at the unwanted intrusion.

"Listen to me and listen carefully!" Truong ordered. "This is Sidewinder. Do you know that word? *Sidewinder!* Do you understand me now?"

"Y-yes..." the young man on the other end of the line stammered. "Yes...yes! Sidewinder... You pay the bills around here and—"

Someone else was grabbing the phone away. A woman's voice soothed his rage. "Sidewinder? This is Coral. I was told you might call."

"You are Phi-Chau, woman?"

"Yes. Phi-Chau Gang. You know that."

"I do?"

"This is safehouse. You have phone number. You know."

"Ah, good...very good. Yes, you are well trained. You will do fine," Truong said, his voice crackling with a sinister chuckle. "Very well. I want you to copy down these cities."

"Cities?"

He could hear her stalling for time as she groped for a pen or pencil. "Yes, my sweet little thing. Seven cities, and the zip codes to go with them—for confirmation. I want you to inform Boa immediately. Phi-Chau is to give me its immediate and total assistance in this matter."

"Of course, Sidewinder."

"In doing this you will not only be helping me and mine, you will be tasting revenge for some of your own dead."

Truong laughed to himself. The Vietnamese government bankrolled the Phi-Chau Gang in San Francisco and the Vietnamese Association in New York. Hanoi employed the Phi-Chau to do its dirty work wherever Vietnamese refugees were involved. It was better that the police think there was a criminal element involved in certain street murders, and not a political connection. The Association couldn't be implicated. And the Phi-Chau had become very trustworthy after that first year when a few of its members had rebelled and Truong himself had had to deliver a head or two to their clubhouse to show Hanoi's seriousness. Now that the Vietnamese Secret Police financed most of Phi-Chau's activities, the gang's cooperation was guaranteed, although Truong had needed their services less and less lately. But now . . . now that Able Team was about to hit the four corners of the country, his manpower reserves would be stretched to the limit, if not beyond. It was better to dispatch Phi-Chau's brother gangsters throughout the United States to assist him in this matter. And if they got a little overzealous and began blowing away American commandos? Well, Truong couldn't be everywhere at the same time now, could he?

That thought brought another smile to the major's lips.

Sidewinder, Boa, Coral. The Phi-Chau clan was named for its members' love of snakes. Both Truong and Hanoi found it amusing, and the hierarchy back in Vietnam had ordered Truong to use the reptilian titles as long as the Vietnamese Secret Police was dealing with the gang. The gang members themselves had been using the nicknames since the group's formation nearly ten years earlier.

"Start getting your people together," he advised the woman known as Coral. "Have them prepared to move out on a moment's notice."

"We will be waiting for further directives, Sidewinder."

"I will contact you this afternoon. From Denver."

THE DUAL-PROP AIRLINER Carl Lyons and the others were riding over the mountaintops and down into Denver was so small that the group felt every bump and dip of turbulence that had begun the moment their pilot had announced he was beginning his descent into Mile High City. When the Able Team warriors finally started down the stairs to the solid tarmac below, there was no one in the group who was without a clenched jaw or white knuckles. "I *hate* coming to this town," Schwarz declared, shaking his head from side to side. "Always have. Always will."

"Ah, but you miss Colorado Springs, don't you?" Blancanales gibed, elbowing him. "Remember the Black Cat Saloon just outside Fort Carson?"

"How could I forget?" Gadgets said, grinning as his knees stopped wobbling.

"Maybe we could pay the joint a visit—for old times' sake. *After* the mission."

"Gentlemen," Lyons said, his gesture reminding them both that there was a woman weaving down the stairs behind them.

"Don't mind me," Haley said, laughing. "I'm just happy to be alive!"

Klein had requested a week's leave of absence from the SFPD, to be subtracted from the accrued compensation time she'd been saving up. Her supervisor had been reluctant to grant it on such short notice, but a quick phone call from Chief of Detectives Crowe got everything straightened out.

"Good old one-oh-one," Lyons said, glancing at his wristwatch after spotting a white Plymouth cross the runway and approach them. Red and blue lights flashed atop its roof.

"One-oh-one?" Blancanales asked.

"Car 101," Lyons said, motioning toward the Plymouth's license plates. The numbers *101* were emblazoned in jet-black across a plain white field under the words State Patrol. "I phoned ahead," Ironman explained. "Arranged for my old buddy Nightstick Nick to meet us here, escort us around Denver and get us over to the zoo ASAP!"

"You sure don't believe in keeping a low profile, do you?" Klein commented as the all-white four-door with a "flying wheel" emblem on both sides slid up in front of Able Team. Behind the wheel a highway patrolman wearing mirrored sunglasses and an ear-to-ear grin nodded back eagerly at Ironman.

"Oh-oh," Blancanales groaned as he glanced over at Schwarz. "These two look *too* happy."

"Like they're definitely up to something," Gadgets added.

"Me and ol' Nick truly kicked some ass last time I was out this way in an...*official* capacity with the LAPD," Lyons explained. "The brass had me out here checking on a threat to the California governor. The radicals making the threat also had Colorado's governor on their death list. Nightstick Nick was one of the governor's bodyguards back then. Looks like they've got him working the street again. Back in the bag."

"The bag?" Schwarz said, frowning.

"Uniform," Haley supplied with a smile. She knew *that* slang.

Leaving the rumbling Plymouth was a clean-shaven patrolman in his early thirties. He was slender but agile, and shorter than Lyons. His brown hair was close-cropped, though Lyons knew that the strands creeping adventurously over the edge of his ears might be grounds for a reprimand letter if his supervisor spotted them. He could also be called on the carpet for leaving his hat inside the car instead of wearing it everywhere, as Colorado State Patrol rules and regulations dictated. Nightstick Nick didn't seem to be intimidated by a law-enforcement bureaucracy's bible of infractions, however.

"Thanks for meeting us," Lyons said, extending a meaty fist.

"My pleasure, my pleasure!" Nightstick Nick popped open the trunk before shaking everyone's hand. "What, no luggage? Those old biddies from the Welcome Wagon kind of frown on one-night stands, you know." He grinned slyly, eyeballing Haley Klein.

"Uh, we're traveling kind of light this time through," Lyons explained.

"And we're kind of in a hurry," Blancanales said, his tone telling the highway patrolman he hoped the man was aware this wasn't to be a tourists' cruise through downtown.

"I kind of figured that," Nightstick Nick said, gesturing toward his flashing sonic bar. "Hoped I'd be here sooner. Hoped I'd be waiting for you when you arrived, but Dispatch had me working a triple-fatal on the north side of metro. Propane truck versus locomotive."

"Metro-North. Your old stomping grounds?" Lyons asked.

"Naw," the officer said as he took their two tote bags and gently placed them in the trunk between first-aid satchels, a crate of shotgun ammo and a spare snow tire with steel studs protruding from the rubber. "One suburb to the west. The Thornton Thumpers there were all tied up with a barricade-hostage situation. So who does that leave to handle the traffic crap?" His thumbs tapped the outline of his concealed body armor. "State, of course."

"Nightstick Nick hates working for the state police," Lyons informed the others.

"Traffic sucks," Nightstick Nick agreed.

"He's testing for the Denver PD," Ironman explained. "Wants to be a real cop."

"Not a meter maid with a gun."

"He's on the DPD's waiting list. Seven years and counting."

"Meantime, I go where I want to go," Nightstick Nick said, smiling. "And right now I'm off the clock, so we go wherever *you* want to go. Ten-thirty-nine."

"Ten-thirty-nine?" Haley asked as she got into the back seat between Blancanales and Schwarz.

"Lights and Siren."

"They don't use simple civilian cop talk out here," Lyons said. "They use the ten code."

Nightstick Nick nodded. "Real antiquated. Had to practically file a civil suit just to get the chief to let us trash the cross-draw holsters. They used to be mandatory here, you know."

"You're kidding," Klein gasped.

"No. Real wild West mentality—only every time the guys quick-drawed, they tended to shoot whoever was standing slightly off to their left—bad guy *or* good. Where to?"

"The zoo," Lyons said without a smile.

"Denver County Jail?" Nightstick Nick flipped the siren selector from yelp mode to high-low and turned on the sonic bar.

Lyons just laughed.

17

Gadgets Schwarz examined the wolves' cage from every possible angle, but there was no section or segment that might have been used by One-eyed Ngoc or his Cult of Seven to hide additional clues leading to the recovery of ten million dollars in emeralds or misappropriated documents.

Even Nightstick Nick's legendary driving skills hadn't been enough to get Able Team to the Denver Zoo by the closing time, and thus Lyons and his people had been unable to question the head zoo keeper or his staff about the wolves or their concrete-and-wrought-iron lair. The on-duty guard was new, lazy and uncooperative.

There were only two wolves in the thirty-by-forty-outdoor pit. They were ruggedly beautiful animals that stood three feet tall at the shoulders. Their lower jaws hung open, exposing sharp fangs and incisors and their unblinking eyes glowed an eerie rain-forest green as they closely inspected every move the five humans made.

"There's nothing inside this cage," Blancanales said after he and Schwarz had walked around it nearly a half-dozen times, searching for clues.

"And nothing down in the lair itself," Schwarz said. "Just some tree trunks, slabs of concrete, a feeding tray, that little creek and the lair itself."

"And we ain't goin' in *there*," Klein said, forcing a tense laugh as she locked eyes with Lyons. "Are we?"

"You and the wolves have the same kind of green eyes," Ironman teased. "Maybe they'd let *you* inside for a little visit."

"We could give you one of grandma's little cookie baskets to take along," Gadgets said, winking as he licked his chops with mock menace.

"You guys are too much," she said, hugging herself against the chill of nightfall. As a crescent moon slowly rose above the roof of the lion house on the other side of the zoo's main footpath, both wolves began to howl.

"Bingo!" Blancanales suddenly called.

Thinking he had made some connection between the howling of the wolves and the case they were trying to solve, Lyons and Klein raced Schwarz over to the section of wall paneling Politician was examining with a flashlight. "What is it?" Klein asked.

"Graffiti," Blancanales said, tapping a rigid forefinger against several signatures carved into the wooden planks.

"Graffiti?"

"This section in particular," he answered, allowing the flashlight beam to play over a section of wood decorated with deep carvings that seemed to come together in the shape of Vietnamese words.

"What does it mean?" Klein asked the Able Team commandos.

"How would I know?" Blancanales replied with a shake of his head. "I just find the clues. *You* guys get to figure them out."

"*Phi-Chau con gau ao chuom?*" Schwarz said, trying to pronounced the unfamiliar words.

"I'll phone the Denver PD," Lyons said as he scanned the empty zoo for a pay phone or information center. "They've got a sizable Little Saigon of their own here on Federal Boulevard. They're bound to have a translator or interpreter at police headquarters."

"No need," Nightstick Nick said. He was jotting the words down in a pocket notebook. Once completed, he added, "Wait one," and ran back to his car, which he'd parked on the other side of the fence, three hundred feet away.

"Won't his sergeant be wondering where that unit is right now?" Schwarz asked Ironman.

"Naw. Each patrolman in District One is assigned his own patrol car. Sometimes two men to a car, but hot dogs like Nightstick Nick ride solo. They're too gung-ho. The old-timers can't stand 'em. And the rookies can't stomach all the action. His sergeant is probably just glad Car 101 is nowhere to be seen or heard from at this point in time."

"Why do you say that?"

"New sergeants screw with Nightstick Nick only once. When they taste his brand of retaliation, they learn their lesson fast, and usually request a transfer to Gunnison."

"Okay, so everyone cool it," Lyons said. "Here he comes."

Chest heaving, Nightstick Nick was still carrying his pocket notebook. And something else—a tiny dictionary. "It was in my briefcase," he said, revealing the cover: *Romanized English-Vietnamese Dictionary*.

"I've got ones in Thai, Chinese, Japanese and Khmer back in the car, too. Hardly ever use any except for the Viet one, though."

"Let me see that!" Gadgets demanded. Within a few seconds he'd translated the graffiti. Phi-Chau, of course, stood for the notorious Vietnamese gang, which they all knew. "*Con gau*...and *ao chuom*," he mumbled under his breath. And then his eyes rose from Nightstick Nick's pocket dictionary and began scanning the nearby cages of other wild animals. "Over there," he said, pointing on the run.

Straight for the polar bear pit.

"Whatever it is, it's waiting for us down there in that pond," Gadgets told the others after they'd crossed the narrow footpath and gathered alongside the polar bear pit.

"Luckily it's only October," Blancanales said, crossing himself. When the others looked at him with questioning eyes, he quickly added, "Otherwise, whatever it is that's waiting for us down there would be waiting under a thick layer of ice."

"He's probably right," Nightstick Nick said.

Unlike the wolves' cage, which was situated on level ground, the polar bear pit was exactly that—a pit. Forty feet straight down three polar bears shared a fifty-by-fifty-foot den of sculptured concrete shielded by high brick walls on all sides and protruding bars along the top. The bars protected the people from the bears. Chain-link fencing, supplemented with generous layers of chicken wire, served to protect the bears from the people.

Currently none of the huge animals were visible. "They're probably lurking inside that mock cave over there," Haley said, pointing to a dark crevice forty feet away from the man-made pond. "Who's going to go down there and find out?"

"How deep does the pond look to you?" Lyons asked Schwarz.

"Well, it's crystal-clear. Based on that boulder lying on the bottom, and those other objects along the edge there— where they've got the little fake frogman and his treasure chest display set up—about twenty feet deep, max."

"Little frogman and treasure chest?" Klein questioned.

Gadgets handed her his set of folding binoculars. "I've no idea why it's down there," he said, pointing. "The zoo visitors can't really see it from up here."

"Maybe it placates the polar bears," Blancanales muttered.

"Are you guys really serious about going down there?" Nightstick Nick asked.

"Does a polar bear sneeze?" Pol quipped.

"Well, it's none of my business," the state patrolman said, ignoring Blancanales and turning to Lyons, "but if *I* needed to search that thing down there for whatever it is you guys are after, I'd wait until morning and have the zoo people transfer the big bad bears to another pit or something."

"We're sort of running against the clock on this one," Schwarz said. "And, besides, something like that would attract too much attention. Word would get out—there'd be a media blitz."

"And if we haven't already been followed to Denver," Lyons began, "they'd probably hear about it soon enough on TV and board the next flight to Colorado."

"In that case, I know a guy who can get down there, in and out, in record time," Nick advised them. "He just loves challenges."

"Does he have a security clearance?" Ironman asked.

"How does Adams County Sheriff's Department Underwater Rescue Squad sound?"

Ironman frowned. "Diver?"

"Yep," Nightstick Nick said, his eyes glazing with envy.

"How soon can you get him out here, and without the whole metro-wide network of news media guys monitoring the call?" Lyons asked.

"I don't even have to trot back to my car," Nightstick Nick answered as he produced a quarter and pointed at the pay phone. "Fifty Fathoms Fred just happens to be my roommate."

Below, a thunderous growl diverted their attention. Two of the polar bears had appeared at the mouth of their artificial cave. Soon a cub waddled out between them.

"Oh, how cute," Haley said, giggling.

"Shit!" Blancanales said, shaking his head. "'Cute,' she says. You'll be cute if we send you down there to entertain them while the sheriff's divers do their thing, won't you?"

"Hey, mellow out, Politician," Lyons said quickly. "I just wonder if that cub's number three, or if baby makes four."

THE THREE BEARS had retreated back into their cave by the time Nightstick Nick's roommate showed up an hour later. He wore only the lower half of a wet suit and dragged his goggles and oxygen tank behind him.

Sergeant Fred Diablo was a twenty-year veteran of the Sheriff's Department. He was as tall as Lyons but stockier, with an extra twenty pounds of rock-hard muscle on his chest. His hair was short, reddish-brown and sparse, like the bristles of a steel brush. His eyes bulged and his lips seemed constantly pursed, as if he were inside a pressurized water tank that was about to burst.

"You want me to go down *where*?" he asked, his eyes bulging even more when Lyons pointed at the sign advertising three polar bears.

"Don't worry!" Nightstick Nick consoled him. Nick now brandished a 12-gauge shotgun with folding stock. "I'll cover you, partner."

"That piece of shit ain't gonna stop no polar bear, bro."

"I wasn't going to *shoot* him," Nick replied, producing an injured expression. "I was going to shoot in *front* of him—just scare him back into his cave if he comes out."

"Yeah, *if*, my ass," Diablo returned as he surveyed the edge of the pit. "More like *when*, you mean! They're sniffin' at our scent right now, girls . . . just waiting. They know we're up to no good."

"Your balls are just shrinking, Fred, that's all," Nightstick Nick challenged with a hearty laugh.

"Quiet!" Diablo was leaning over the pit's edge again, gauging the distance between the iron railing and the pond's surface.

"You'll wake the bears up again!" Schwarz agreed.

"How do you plan to lower my ass down there?" Diablo asked.

Haley lifted a long coil of fire hose. "This should enable you to submerge without even a splash," she explained. "We'll tie it around you and lower you slowly until you're in the water."

"Then you just keep the hose near," Lyons went on, "until you find what we want. Then get back to the hose, hang on—"

"And we'll hoist your unworthy ass back up!" Nightstick Nick finished.

"Shit!" Fifty Fathoms Fred said, frowning. "So what am I looking for, anyway? A body or what?"

"We're not sure," Lyons said, shrugging.

"You're not *what*?" Diablo's eyes began bulging again.

"Just get down there," Nightstick Nick said, "and scour the bottom. Let us know if you find anything... suspicious."

"Right," Ironman said.

"And we'll go on from there," Schwarz said.

Deputy Fred Diablo was floating silently across the surface of the polar bear pond less than five minutes later, his waterproof flashlight sending powerful beams back and forth through the murky water as his flippered feet rose and fell in slow motion, powering him along. Now and then he would dive slowly. Nightstick Nick kept the front shotgun sight trained on the entrance to the bears' cave the whole time. Every few minutes a rumbling growl would rise from the artificial cave, but the polar bears never emerged.

An hour into the search Fifty Fathoms Fred exploded above the surface. "Could this be it?" he asked, holding out a metal file box about the size of an alarm clock, obviously waterproof and equipped with a rust-resistant lock.

"Throw it up here!" Blancanales yelled down at him.

"Hold it down, guys!" Lyons warned them.

"Holy shit!" Deputy Diablo threw the file box up over the pit's edge, then began frantically swimming for the fire hose: no one had known—and Fifty Fathoms Fred hadn't yet discovered—that a portion of the polar bears' cave was connected to a subterranean passageway that emptied out beneath the surface of the pond.

The male polar bear—largest of the three—was now swimming wildly underwater, directly toward the deputy sheriff.

18

"Fire into the center of the pool!" Lyons yelled at Nightstick Nick. "Fire directly into the center of the—"

A deafening discharge drowned out Ironman's words as a blinding flash left the muzzle of Nightstick Nick's 12-gauge shotgun. Then another, and another—the state patrolman's gun arm pumping a fresh cartridge in to replace each spent shell.

The blasts of double-aught buckshot struck the surface of the pond three or four feet in front of the bear's snout, sending great geysers of bubbles and steel pellets down into the pool. But they didn't dissuade the bear from reaching his goal.

Diablo flew up out of the water and grabbed the fire hose with one hand. He waved his other hand frantically, hoping the momentum would help swing him out of the animal's reach when it surfaced. "Take me, you crazy bastards! Take me up!"

Just as the polar bear erupted through the surface—front paws clawing wildly at the flying froth and suds, jaws outstretched, snout aiming for Diablo's rear end—the frogman was plucked from the fangs of death.

And then the fire hose snapped in two at its couplings!

"Oh, my God!" Fifty Fathoms Fred cried out as he was dunked back into the polar bear pool like a human cannonball.

By now a groggy female polar bear had ambled out onto the ledge of her artificial cave, testing the cool night breeze with an uplifted snout. It didn't take her long to figure out what was going on, and she charged into the pool, too. Fully a quarter of the man-made pond's water seemed to leave the basin when the monstrous female completed her clumsy dive.

"I'm out of ammo! I'm out of ammo!" Nightstick Nick began yelling, although he was still pumping away with his shotgun and filling the night with fiery 12-gauge explosions. And then he slid the last cartridge into the Ithaca.

"Where's the file box?" Gadgets Schwarz yelled. Schwarz was running back and forth, searching the iron bars that curled around the pit's edge. "Where's the file box! I saw him throw that sucker up here! Where's the goddamn file box!"

"Screw the file box!" Nightstick Nick roared. He had set down his shotgun and was now climbing out onto the protective fence. "We gotta help my buddy!" He drew an S&W Model 28 revolver.

"Don't jump down in there!" Lyons ordered as a chorus of sirens grew in the distance. "Whatever you do, don't jump down in there. Do you hear?"

"Here!" Haley yelled as she reappeared out of the darkness. She was dragging another fire hose behind her.

"Come on!" Lyons said, directing Blancanales and Schwarz. "Help her get it over the railing there!"

Somehow they got the hose unrolled and lowered to Deputy Diablo, who shinnied up it like a tree monkey chased by two cheetahs through an African jungle. Out of the corner of one eye Lyons saw Nightstick Nick holster his four-inch Smith & Wesson, then draw his billy club and bounce it—long-distance—off the female polar bear's snout.

The great beast clambered up out of the pool, rose on its hind feet and let out an earsplitting roar that seemed to shake the very walls of the bear pit itself. From where Lyons and the others stood, almost directly overhead, the female looked twelve feet tall. From Diablo's vantage point she looked a hundred! And she was closing fast!

Suddenly there was a flapping of giant metallic wings overhead, and then the night sky was blocked out by two huge swishing blades as a police helicopter's fifty-foot rotors brought the roaring craft into a hover directly over the zoo. Shifting a few dozen feet to starboard, it quickly floated almost directly over Fifty Fathoms Fred.

If they were wondering what was occurring below their landing skids, the chopper pilot and his DPD observer didn't pause to question the frogman shinnying up out of the zoo's polar bear pit on a fire hose. Instead, they blinded the irate creature with two brilliant spotlights until it backed off and retreated to its growling spouse and whining cub.

"Here it is!" Haley said, scooping up the file box from a plot of ferns as Schwarz and Blancanales grabbed a trembling Deputy Diablo and dragged him away from his showdown with the polar bear.

"You guys . . . saved me!" Diablo cried out with a long, drawn-out sigh, feigning semiconsciousness as hugs were exchanged.

"Of course we did, bro!" Nightstick Nick said, trying to slap him out of it. "Nobody else would have—and remember that! Now let's all get over to my car before the cavalry shows up and we have to explain why we were messing with the poor polar bears so late at night!" Overhead, the police chopper swooped back and forth, buzzing two spitting gorillas in the giant outdoor monkey refuge that rose behind the polar bear pit.

"They'll just think it was a Colorado State Patrol choir practice that got out of control!" Lyons said, laughing.

"Naw, they know us better than that!" Nightstick Nick said. "Too many prudes on the force."

"And I think I know how you got the nickname Nightstick Nick!" Schwarz said, slapping the patrolman on the back as they trotted toward his cruiser and dozens of Denver police cars began streaming into the zoo from a side gate on the opposite side of the polar bear pit. "Did you see the way he bounced his billy club off that monster's snout back there?" Gadgets asked Blancanales.

"Yeah, I felt kind of bad about having to do that!" Nightstick Nick said. "I'm an animal lover from way back you know. But I read somewhere that if you get attacked by a grizzly, just fall down, roll up and play dead. If they bite into you, pound on their snout and repeat steps one, two and three."

NIGHTSTICK NICK LIVED on the twenty-ninth floor of Broox Towers, one of downtown Denver's highest apartment buildings. The penthouse suite, topping the forty-second floor, was rumored to be leased exclusively to the blond, buxom country singer Dolly Parton.

The patrolman's one-bedroom unit had a balcony that took up the entire north wall and overlooked Mile High City's skyline, as well as some suburbs to the north. The walls of his den were covered with framed certificates from nearly every police and sheriff's department in the metropolitan area—certificates of appreciation and recognition.

Gadgets looked closely, but he could find none from the patrolman's own agency. "They're the *real* reason everyone calls him Nightstick Nick," Deputy Diablo explained. "Nick carries an eight-channel scanner in his cruiser. State patrolmen can cruise just about anywhere. They have countywide districts for the most part. Nick tired quickly of writing speeding tickets and diagraming fender benders. When he wasn't running thousands of abandoned auto VINs through the headquarters computer on graveyard shift, he was out and about, cruising the major intercity arteries, responding to calls for help from the suburban PDs...even Denver's northern districts."

"I got addicted to it," Nightstick Nick admitted. "Once the old billy club came out, it was difficult to stop. That letter of reprimand over there *is* from my department—from my sergeant," he said, pointing to a CSP letterhead hanging on the far wall.

"A *framed* letter of *reprimand*?" Schwarz said, gulping incredulously.

"Yeah. From one of my sergeants who'd memorized the book. He got pissed off 'cause I took forty-five minutes to get to a fender bender. Big deal. I was down in Five Points, helpin' DPD Metro kick ass and take names."

"But you *frame* your letters of reprimand?" Schwarz pressed.

"Only the better ones. The ones that get a laugh or bring back good memories. The ones that make my sergeants out to look like meter maids undeserving of the service revolver on their hips. Yeah, sometimes the reprimands make me proudest. And it wasn't the citizens who complained about me," Nightstick Nick said, laughing. "My *sergeant* did." He read from the framed letter of reprimand. "'And Patrolman so-and-so was found to be out of his assigned patrol area, responding to an officer-needs-help call when he had previously been assigned to handle a noninjury traffic accident at Fifty-second and Washington instead.' What a crock. It doesn't mention here that a Denver officer *died* during that officer-needs-help call, and that I was closer to it than the traffic accident."

"Sometimes sergeants just have their heads up their asses," Lyons said. Lyons had been fiddling with the locked file box for a good half hour now, trying to pry it open with one of the state patrolman's old Saigon souvenirs: a K-bar blade.

"Yeah? Well, screw 'em," Nightstick Nick said, folding his arms across his chest victoriously.

"Imagine that," Ironman said, still shaking his head "Placing a traffic accident above an officer-needs-help call."

"You ever invite this Sergeant Klaxman up here to eye-ball your awards gallery?" Blancanales asked, the tilt to his eyes saying he wasn't impressed as he read the signature on one of the letters of reprimand.

"Naw," Nightstick Nick answered, glancing out the window. "We don't get along much off duty."

"I'll tell you *one* dude who ought to get a letter of commendation for tonight's action on the field of battle!" Fifty Fathoms Fred declared as he waved a forefinger in the air.

"Who?" Nightstick Nick asked with mock humility.

"Jumpin' Joe Padilla!"

"That DPD chopper jock?"

"Yep!"

"You'll be lucky if Jumpin' Joe don't come on over here after his shift's up and jump down our throats!"

"Why?"

"For skipping out on him back there like that without an explanation."

"All I know is that I was being chased by a damn polar bear, and then out of the blue comes a police chopper, so close I can see Jumpin' Joe and his PD-blue sunglasses and his ear-to-ear grin. Yeah, Jumpin' Joe's got my vote!"

"Ah, finally," Lyons sighed. He had succeeded in prying open the file box.

"What the hell?" Blancanales murmured. He reached in and removed a tightly wrapped bundle of oil-smeared waterproof wax paper. Inside was a handful of small key and a grainy black-and-white photograph.

"Seven of them," Schwarz observed.

"Those are postal box keys," Haley told them. She opened the top button of her blouse, reached in and brough out a similar key on the end of a sterling silver neck chain "I've got one just like it."

"Who's the photo of?" Fifty Fathoms Fred asked.

"Ho Chi Minh," Blancanales said, his lips curling in disgust.

"The old VC leader?" Nightstick Nick asked, moving in for a closer look.

"Former president of North Vietnam," Blancanales confirmed. "Died in 1969."

"What's this?" Haley asked as she ran her fingernail along the yellowing snapshot. Ho Chi Minh's hands had been circled in what appeared to be red lipstick.

No one had an answer just yet. Instead, they all turned their attention to the keys. Each one had a five-digit number engraved on it, just like Haley's. "The number of the P.O. box," she explained.

"Am I to assume each one of these keys unlocks a P.O. box in one of the seven cities unscrambled from the thirty-five-digit code by Kurtzman back at Stony Man Farm?" Blancanales asked, locking eyes with Lyons.

Lyons nodded. "It's all we've got to go on. Which city comes first?"

"Freeport, Maine," Blancanales answered, scanning the list. "Followed by Hilton Head, South Carolina; Plymouth, Massachusetts; Angel Fire, New Mexico; Greenwich Village, New York; Montpelier, Vermont; and Little Torch Key, Florida," he reminded them.

"New York?" Nightstick Nick said, his eyes lighting up. "I always wanted to go there, Ironman. Hell, we could have a good ol' street-stompin' shit-kicker of a time!"

"I'm afraid *you* and Deputy Diablo aren't going anywhere," Lyons said, thrusting his jaw out.

"What?" Fifty Fathoms Fred exclaimed, standing up and lifting both fists in front of his glaring face.

"You two have done an excellent job here," Lyons said, somewhat amused, "and we appreciate it. But now your people need you back at your respective departments."

"Forget it," Nightstick Nick sneered.

"And we've got to get a move on," Lyons continued. "The fewer cooks in the kitchen the better. Hell, I should even send Haley here packing back to the SFPD."

"But you need at least one pretty face in the mob scene, right?" Klein taunted confidently. "As a bargaining chip for tight times, if nothing else."

"Something like that."

"We'll need a lift back over to the airport, though," Blancanales said. "We've got a Lear jet to catch." He glanced across the room at Nightstick Nick. "Can do?"

"Sure thing, pal."

"Where to first?" Gadgets asked Ironman.

"What was that town in New Mexico again?" Ironman asked Politician.

"Angel Fire."

"Village on the edge of doomsday," Schwarz said cryptically.

"What?" Blancanales questioned.

"Nothing. Just a dream I had once."

IF MAJOR TRUONG HAD KNOWN that Nightstick Nick had put a thousand odd dollars of his own personal paycheck into reinforcing Car 101 with a pursuit package and inner roll bar, he might not have chosen to broadside the vehicle at such a slow speed, even with the powerful four-wheel-drive truck he was driving.

Truong had followed Able Team from the Denver Zoo to Broox Towers. He'd watched Nightstick Nick pull into the underground garage in the heart of downtown Denver. He'd watched the CSP officer hand one of the security guards five dollars to watch the car, nonstop, until they got back. And then Truong had backtracked two blocks, stolen the truck and brought it back down into the garage.

His strategy was to park near the entrance and wait for the patrol car to exit again. He would ram it from the side as it started up the only access ramp—ram it right into a generator plastered with huge red-and-yellow Danger—High Voltage signs.

It didn't quite work out that way. Instead of crushing the Plymouth, the four-wheel-drive truck all but bounced off the reinforced frame—Truong hadn't built up enough momentum prior to impact.

The first instinct of every person inside the patrol car was to respond with a trigger-fanning display of drawn pistols. But they were in the heart of the city, and the accident might prove to be a simple traffic mishap. Steam from the truck's hissing radiator quickly filled the underground garage. And by the time they realized what had really happened, Truong escaped in all the confusion.

19

Angel Fire was an enchanting spot. Sleek white slopes surrounded the city, which became the first stop on Able Team's list of seven out-of-the-ordinary zip codes.

To get to Angel Fire, Able Team's Lear jet first had to land at a secret government runway located in the rolling prairies midway between San Cristobal and Red River, New Mexico.

From there they rented a Jeep and raced down through the Sangre de Cristo Mountains, where black bear, elk and deer paused alongside the winding roadways, or sometimes directly on the median line itself. After the polar bear pit at the Denver Zoo, these additional encounters with nature were a bit too much for Blancanales. He said nothing, but Lyons and Schwarz could both see it in his eyes. The guy longed for the concrete jungle of Los Angeles.

They passed ghost towns and old abandoned gold mines at high speed. Jasmine clung to logs along the roadsides, and sunflower petals were cast onto the lingering snowbanks by the blast of tail wind from their speeding Jeep.

On Highway 38, eighteen miles east of Red River, they roared through Eagle's Nest, a laid-back resort with a particularly deep lake. But the commandos of Able Team hardly noticed the scenery. Besides, it was pretty dark out now.

Finally they found Angel Fire, another eleven miles to the south. The post office was a double-wide trailer affair, with aluminum paneling to help cut down on heating bills. Someone had commissioned an artist to paint forest scenery on the drab structure, but he or she had done a dismal job, and much of the mural had been whitewashed over in anticipation of a much-needed fresh coat of simple brown or beige.

A mile uproad from the post office access road a red VW van pulled in behind Able Team's rented Jeep. It followed at low speed, keeping a half-dozen car lengths between the two vehicles.

"We've got trouble," Lyons muttered to Schwarz, who was driving.

"Trouble with a capital *T*," Blancanales added as a blue station wagon pulled in behind the Volkswagen van.

"Think we can handle that many?" Lyons asked.

"Depends on the number of shooters."

"Stand by," Klein said as she pulled out her makeup mirror. "I'm getting a head count right now."

"Do I pull into the post office or drive by?" Schwarz asked.

"Pull in," Lyons directed. "Let's see what happens."

"Maybe we should cruise on down to that bend in the road and unload on them," Blancanales suggested. "If we stop here, innocent people might get hurt."

"There's nobody around this late at night," Lyons argued. "The place is deserted. The box section might not even be open!"

"Screw it," Gadgets said, swerving into the postal office parking lot. "I'm tired of games with no payoff."

The driver of the VW van doused his headlights and coasted into a parking spot several dozen feet away. Inside the van gun barrels took shape as men moved about, preparing to exit.

"There's an AK silhouette," Blancanales warned.

"This is it," Lyons announced. "Lock and load, ladies."

Then there was an earsplitting roar as the blue station wagon skidded up into the parking lot. Sliding sideways, it came to rest between Able Team's Jeep and the VW van. A half-dozen men clad in black coveralls—all armed with Colt AR-15 assault rifles—jumped out, their barrels aimed at the windows of the Volkswagen.

"Sheriff's Department!" someone shouted through a bullhorn. "Everyone out of this side of the vehicle, hands in the air, no weapons, or you're leftovers for the meat wagon!"

"Sheriff's Department?" Blancanales repeated, glancing over at Lyons.

Slack-jawed, Lyons and the others watched five Vietnamese males slowly step from the van and lie facedown in the parking lot. Flashlight beams penetrated the vehicle, but there was no one else hiding inside.

"Stow the hardware," Lyons whispered. "Under that blanket, back seat floorboard. Let me do the talking. Nobody mention the mission unless they discover the guns—at which time I'll *still* do all the talking."

"It's your ball game," Gadgets muttered.

After the deputies took all five of the Asians into custody for weapons violations, a big, barrel-chested man with gray whiskers and a glowing cigar dangling over the edge of his lower lip strode up to them, smile growing. "Evening folks!" he said, treating them to a semicasual half salute.

"What's going on, Officer?" Lyons asked.

"I'm afraid I'm going to have to request some form of ID from you all," the lawman replied. "We spotted these fellows here five days ago, camping out on the hillside, target shooting and acting generally subversive toward nature. Had one of my men watching them real close. Tonight they made their move. I don't know if they were planning to rob you folks or what! But you're lucky we were here to intervene."

"You're so right, Officer!" Haley said, leaning forward, her attractive face beaming from the Jeep's cramped back seat.

"Tourists?" the peace officer asked as he collected Able Team's phony ID cards.

"These two are," Lyons said, pointing to Blancanales and Schwarz. "I'm in from the military, visiting my folks. She's my sister!" he said, gesturing toward Haley.

"I don't have any ID with me," she cooed helplessly, "but I *do* have a P.O. box inside there if you want to come and check me out!" Still smiling, Klein held out her box key.

"Oh, I don't think that'll be necessary!" the officer said, laughing jovially. "You look pretty trustworthy. Now what's your date of birth, honey?"

"Here," Haley said, handing Lyons her key. "Go and check the box while I talk with the officer here."

Nodding, he took the key and trotted over to the post office. One of the front entryway glass doors was locked, and a bolt of anxiety shot through his gut, but the other door was open and he rushed in, stomping his boots as if to rid himself of the chill.

The box was easy to locate. It was on his immediate right, a dozen rows up from the ground. He removed the seven keys from his front pocket, inserted the correct one and thought of booby traps only after he began twisting. But there was no explosion.

Inside, he found a handful of junk mail addressed to Occupant and a bright green envelope with nothing written on the outside and no postage affixed. Glancing over his shoulder to make sure none of the deputies were approaching, he slit open the envelope and poured the contents into the palm of his hand, a simple sliver of paper with three words scrawled across it in red lipstick: *Cai Den Tho*.

"This is getting stranger by the minute," he muttered under his breath before returning to the crisp New Mexican night air.

"Hands on top of your head, young fellow," someone ordered, poking a shotgun barrel into the small of his back. "Interlock your fingers and don't make no funny moves."

Lyons stared at the Jeep. His companions were all spread-eagled on the ground beside it. Several New Mexico State Police cars were swooping down into the parking lot, which was now ablaze with flashing red lights.

The friendly peace officer had found their collection of exotic weapons on the floor of the Jeep.

ONE PHONE CALL to Stony Man Farm did the trick. Iron-man had hoped to avoid a hundred questions by playing tourist, but once the deputy saw through his game plan and noticed the firepower stashed inside the Jeep, the Able Team commando was forced to flex his muscles and contact Washington. It all amazed Haley Klein, of course. She had never seen so much red tape dispensed with so rapidly in her brief law-enforcement career.

The Sheriff's Department rescue helicopter—an old Korean War affair, capable of carrying a dozen wounded GIs— ferried Able Team back to their Lear jet, saving a great deal of time. It was then simply a matter of four or five more hours in the air before the craft touched down in Vermont.

"Just enough time for forty winks," Gadgets said, glancing at his watch. "What time zone are we in?"

"What *town* are we in?" Klein wailed.

"Welcome to Montpelier, folks," Jack Grimaldi announced.

"Montana?" Klein mumbled, rubbing her eyes.

"New England!" Stony Man Farm's crack aircraft pilot corrected, laughing. Grimaldi was capable of handling virtually any sort of plane, fixed wing or otherwise. He'd been pressed into action by Hal Brognola when it had become evident the mission would take Able Team on a cross-country scavenger hunt of sorts.

They landed at the airport near South Barre and took a rental car northbound along an isolated dirt road that meandered alongside the Winooski River for several miles, finally leading back into Montpelier.

The post office was located on an out-of-the-way cul-de-sac hidden at the edge of a business district. Five- and six-story apartment buildings sprouted up all around. Able Team arrived shortly after sunrise.

The post office counter wasn't yet open, but the P.O. box section remained available to the public twenty-four hours a day and, after driving past and parking two blocks down the street, Blancanales returned on foot to get a feel for the place. If there were Phi-Chau gangsters waiting for them in New Mexico of all places, they could just as conceivably show up here in Vermont.

It didn't take Politician long to spot the dark green Cadillac with the New York license plates. Its windows were tinted, but while he was watching from the shadows of a tree line an Asian male in his early twenties, wearing a black trench coat and slicked-back, shoulder-length hair, emerged from the vehicle, walked to the back and began urinating.

Without being noticed, Blancanales returned to Lyons and the others and reported what he had observed.

"Maybe they're just waiting for the post office to open," Haley said.

"Yeah, maybe they're waiting to mail some pirated computer software back to the homeland," Schwarz snapped sarcastically.

"Let's do it, then," Haley said, stepping out of the car.

Exchanging semiamused smirks, Lyons and the others circled around on foot, hoping to get a drop on the gunmen, one of whom was loitering outside the Cadillac. His eyes bulged when he spotted the three men and a woman—all heavily armed—charging him. He exploded into harsh Vietnamese expletives, and the front flaps of his raincoat flew back, revealing an Uzi. An out-of-control burst danced across the sidewalk between Able Team and the Cadillac as the excited Asian struggled to regain control of the barking machine gun.

Lyons and the others all carried CAR-15 assault rifles, capable of unleashing a thirty-round banana clip with blinding speed. Ironman was the first to fire. One single shot. It struck the Asian between the eyes, knocking him backward off his feet and onto the ground. Simultaneously Blancanales blasted the Cadillac's windshield with twenty rounds before releasing his own trigger finger.

Vietnamese gangsters bailed out of the car—some bleeding, all of them screaming unintelligibly—until the vehicle was empty. Even the driver didn't consider fleeing the scene on speeding wheels. The thoughts of every man inside the Cadillac centered on survival—and escaping the ricocheting wasp's nest of hot lead bouncing around inside the automobile.

They all came up shooting.

And Able Team—in combat crouches—responded with additional banana bursts until all the gunmen were lying facedown in the middle of the street, guns suddenly abandoned, hands in plain sight.

Lyons threw Klein one of the P.O. box keys. "Get in there and check it out!" he directed. Turning to Blancanales and Schwarz, he said, "Let's get some IDs off these guys and beat feet!"

In the distance, one, two, then three sirens began wailing. They were all converging on Able Team's location, and Ironman didn't want another confrontation with the law.

Using flexicuffs, he grouped the prisoners back to back and tied each man's elbow to the one beside him. Then he bound their ankles together, making escape impossible. Quickly the weapons were scooped up and thrown into the bullet-riddled Cadillac. Three of the car's tires were flat, but Lyons took the ignition key and pocketed it, anyway.

GRIMALDI'S LEAR JET FLEW them east to Portland, Maine. A hectic eighteen-mile car ride to Freeport followed, during which Lyons opened the green envelope Haley had removed from the post office box in Vermont.

Inside, a single Vietnamese word was scribbled across thin blue stationery. Again in red lipstick: *Bay*.

"Things are getting weird," Blancanales mused.

"This better add up to something good, or I'm gonna personally go after Hal myself," Lyons threatened.

"Any idea what *bay* means in Vietnamese?" Klein asked Blancanales.

"Nope," he said, nodding regretfully. "We should have brought along Nightstick Nick's pocket dictionary."

The post office in Freeport was situated on a wooded hilltop between Bagley House and Amy's Country Kitchen. Built in 1772, Bagley House was the valley's oldest hotel and had served alternately as a church, inn, schoolhouse and trading post over the past two hundred years. Amy's Country Kitchen was a rustic log cabin affair with waitresses dressed in seventeenth-century garb.

As they rattled down the road in their rental car, Lyons suddenly swerved to the side of the road. "Did you see it?" he asked, staring off into the darkness.

"No. What?" Schwarz asked.

"Maybe it was nothing—my imagination."

"What was it?"

"A sparkle...a flash. Up ahead. I don't know."

They had just passed the Muddy Rudder Restaurant, overlooking a sliver of the Cousins River and, in the distant swirling mists, blue herons rose into the murky starlight, frightened by the telltale screech of their car tires.

Located between two long, intersecting tree lines that jutted out from a hillside forest was the post office—a circular two-story affair of modern architecture, topped with several layers of solar paneling. They parked a good hundred feet from the building. Lyons had spotted the telltale gleam of gunmetal somewhere this side of the post office, and he decided they should creep the rest of the way on foot.

"There!" Ironman whispered harshly as he held out a rigid forearm, motioning the rest to drop into silent crouches.

"Yeah, I saw it," Blancanales said, grinning. He brought his CAR-15 up and focused the telescopic sight.

"Treetop sniper?" Schwarz asked, scanning the distant branches, but in the pitch-dark he couldn't see anything.

"Yeah," Pol said, chuckling lightly. "A rifleman leaning back in that patch of rhubarb overlooking the hillside ledge up there." He glanced over his shoulder at Lyons. "Think he's acting suspicious enough to warrant one shot without a warning?"

"Do you see a weapon?" Lyons asked.

Blancanales nodded. "High-powered hunting rifle with a scope. Tryin' to be a pro, I guess."

"Take him out."

"My pleasure."

Blancanales took in a deep breath, exhaled, brought the scope to an inch or so in front of his right eye, then slowly, ever so gently, squeezed the trigger until the weapon seemed to fire itself. There was a slight kick against his shoulder and a dull pop. A heavy thud answered the powerful echo as the round struck the sniper in the left side, nearly tearing his heart out through the jagged exit wound that appeared under the right armpit. The rifleman's lifeless body toppled down the hillside.

"Good shot," Lyons said, patting Pol on the shoulder.

"Of course!" Blancanales replied.

"Let's go!" Gadgets cried, loping off with Haley right behind him.

The sniper was a woman. Lyons rolled her onto her back, revealing pretty features and gruesome wounds. She was slender, tall for an Asian, with high cheekbones. She was also very dead. Her long jet-black hair had been drawn back into a ponytail, but the rubber bands holding it in place had split during the fall, and the silky strands—now casting off a bluish sheen beneath the moonbeams—splayed across her body like an opened Oriental fan.

Lyons patted the dead woman's body down for ID. There was none, of course. And there had been none back at the post office shoot-out in Vermont, either, only the tattoo of a flaring king cobra behind the right ears of the gunmen they had captured.

Suddenly a car engine roared to life several dozen feet away on the other side of the nearest tree line. The car's occupants sped off into the night without even bothering to put up a fight.

"Back to the car?" Gadgets asked. "Want to chase them?"

"Forget it," Lyons said, frowning. "They got the message. Now we get the next piece of the puzzle, then get the hell out of here. I didn't much care for this welcome, and I don't stay long where I'm not wanted."

"Hey, I hear where you're coming from," Blancanales agreed as he wiped down his assault rifle.

A thick green envelope was waiting for them right where it was supposed to be. Inside it was another sliver of light blue stationery. Scrawled in red lipstick were two Vietnamese words: *Ngoi Sao*.

Nearby, sirens filled the night.

20

Plymouth Plantation—a recreated Pilgrim village outside the city of Plymouth, Massachusetts—was a living museum, complete with gardens, houses, farms and architecture representative of 1620s America. The residents relied on diaries, letters, official documents and other writings of the era to portray the lives of actual Pilgrims who arrived on the Mayflower at Plymouth Rock in 1620.

The post office was a temporary affair raised on pillars beside the fort's entrance and decorated more to resemble a cobbler's quaint shoe repair shop than any government operation. Within sight of the post office was a vast field of corn. A hundred-yard-square area a stone's throw from the main fort was cleared annually for a turkey shoot, and the sloping lawns leading to it could be viewed from the post office.

The tourists at the nearby picnic tables had thought nothing of Able Team's arrival until the endless successions of thunderous blasts. The commandos of Able Team drew their weapons and took cover, but the attack was over before they could pinpoint the source of the mortar fire in the nearby forest.

The exploding mortar shells hadn't come close to killing any member of Able Team, although one of the shells had totally destroyed the rental car they'd arrived in and innocents caught in the cross fire had been fatally wounded. Incensed, Able Team scoured the surrounding woods, but it appeared to be a one-barrage attack, compliments of the Phi-Chau Gang again.

The front windows of the old-style post office had been blown out by the shock waves, and a bin loaded with arriving mail was on fire, but the P.O. box section escaped relatively unscathed. Inside the appropriately numbered box another green envelope was quickly located. On the single sliver of blue stationery they found three Vietnamese words this time: *Hoa Son Khau*.

"Any idea what it all means?" Haley asked Ironman and Politician as they hitched a ride back into town while volunteer firemen tried to put out the fires.

"Nope," Pol said, nodding dejectedly. "They could mean just about anything. The words we've been collecting have no hyphenation, no accent marks. In Vietnamese one syllable can have ten different meanings. Without the hyphenation you could go on forever without figuring out what the true meaning might be."

"Then what you're saying is that we're just wasting our time flying from town to town, post office to post office," Gadgets said, scratching his brow.

"Not necessarily," Pol reassured him. "Once we get a collection of words together, someone actually *schooled* in written Vietnamese might be able to make something out of it. Maybe."

"Well, how many places do we have left to check out?" Klein asked.

"Three more," Lyons answered, checking his list. "New York, South Carolina, then down the coast to Florida."

"Which one's next?" Blancanales asked.

"Greenwich Village."

"Then let's do it," Blancanales said.

"Hey, my thumb can only hitch so **much,**" Schwarz groaned.

A farmer driving an old hay wagon pulled over and motioned them onto the back, but the commandos simply stared at one another. "It would be faster to trot back to the airport," Blancanales moaned.

Ironman stared at Haley, who winked back. "No problem," she said, waving the old farmer on.

They watched as she adopted a particularly provocative pose. A souped-up van with two wide-eyed teenagers eager to assist a damsel in distress skidded to the side of the road less than two minutes later. It didn't seem to bother the youths that three rough-looking characters were along for the ride.

THE NARROW, WINDING STREETS of Greenwich Village were a welcome respite to Able Team after the dangerous open spaces of the countryside they'd been forced to traverse the past two days. Here ambushes and sniper attacks seemed less likely—there were simply too many people, too many traffic jams, too much commotion.

Since Saigon Blancanales had found only one other place that could rival the bewitching magic of Tu Do Street—a misty, humid back alley off Waikiki Beach. But here a small segment of side streets ignited that same nostalgic spark in him—if only for a moment. Perhaps it was the balconies from two separate buildings, almost touching, or some artist's unintelligible pop cultural banner hanging from another. The cool October breeze ruined it all, of course. This wasn't the tropics. It was still New York, still the United States of America.

They took a taxi to a corner four blocks from the post office on Kurtzman's list and walked in on foot. Halfway to the main entrance, six young thugs jumped out from an alleyway, brandishing knives, machetes and a baseball bat or two. No firearms were in evidence, but the array of martial arts devices hanging from belts or draped over shoulders was impressive.

"We're not giving donations to the Chinatown Orphanage today, boys," Lyons said without slowing his gait.

One of the youths began swinging a pair of nunchakus. "Revenge for the Phi-Chau brothers killed in San Francisco!" he screamed at the top of his lungs, throwing his head back so that his long black hair flared impressively.

"Revenge!" his cohorts chanted with raised fists and bristling blades.

"How do you want to handle this one, Ironman?" Gadgets asked.

"Enough of this Bruce Lee crap," Blancanales yelled, shaking his head with irritation as he drew the modified Colt .45 hidden in a shoulder holster. Gun arm extended now, he fired at the nearest Vietnamese.

The hollowpoint's devastating punch doubled the man, and he collapsed onto all fours, groaning. Already Politician's pistol was drifting to the left. Another lone discharge, and one of the black-clad baseball players dropped his bat and fell to the filthy sidewalk.

The others whirled, dropped their weapons and fled. Blancanales's automatic rose an inch or two higher as he centered the front sight on a fading point between two bouncing shoulder blades, but the weapon was gently knocked into the air before he could fire.

"Enough," Lyons said simply. "Let's get to the box."

He took key number five and dashed inside the post office. The building was huge, so it took him a good five minutes to locate the correct series of numbers. By that time several police cars had arrived outside, but there had been no witnesses to the one-sided shoot-out.

No one was waiting outside when Ironman emerged from the post office complex, green envelope and an armload of junk mail in hand. But he knew where his men would be: waiting around the corner, engine rumbling.

Five minutes later they were four miles away and heading for the airport. The sliver of blue stationery inside the envelope read simply: *Cai Vinh*.

"I don't know what we're gonna do if one of these P.O. boxes turns up empty," Schwarz said, wiping sweat from his brow as Blancanales swerved onto a main thoroughfare.

"Or one of the boxes ends up closed for nonpayment," Klein said.

"I doubt that'll happen," Lyons said as he stared at the green envelope. "Whoever set this whole thing up—One-eyed Ngoc and his Cult of Seven, if we're to believe what we've found so far—went to too much trouble for a slipup that juvenile."

"Well, I'm keeping my fingers crossed, anyway," Haley said. "Just in case."

"Better to make yourself useful," Pol suggested, handing a half-filled .45 ammo clip back to her. "Fill that sucker up with hollowpoints, will ya?"

A TWO-HOUR FLIGHT to Savannah, then a fifteen-minute ride south to the island of Hilton Head, South Carolina, followed. Lyons was told they would be able to distinguish the unique post office by a red-and-white-striped light-house rising in the distance behind it, due south. Between the lighthouse and the post office would be Broad Creek Lagoon. They'd be able to identify the lagoon by its sail-boats and colorful Windsurfers.

"Well," Schwarz said, "we've covered half the eastern seaboard and all we've got to show for it are five keys and a half-dozen Vietnamese words that don't mean diddly-squat to this veteran code breaker."

"I could use some R & R!" Blancanales said.

"Two more keys, two more words," Haley said sooth-ingly. "Then maybe we'll have enough pieces to put this puzzle together and call it a wrap."

"Yeah, sure...simple," Blancanales grumbled. "I've heard that one before."

They approached the post office on foot from two dif-ferent directions along the coastline after their cabdriver dropped them off within sight of a converted steamboat. If they were expecting something bizarre—frogmen perhaps—all they found was a serene, idyllic setting. No suspicious types loitered in the area. No suspicious cars were parked anywhere to be seen.

But Lyons spotted something out at sea—a schooner lying at anchor several hundred yards offshore. With his folding binoculars he zoomed in on the craft's occupants, who appeared to be enjoying the sunset. "Here," he said, handing the field glasses to Blancanales. "Check 'em out."

Two Asian riflemen, obviously drunk, were reclining on lounge chairs, high-powered hunting rifles balanced across their thighs. A couple of gorgeous bikini-clad women were leaning against the railing, watching the setting sun.

Able Team took full advantage of the situation and were on their way back to the airport before the sun had dropped below the horizon. They took with them the sixth green envelope. Inside were two words: *Anh Trang.*

NEXT ABLE TEAM FLEW to Key West, Florida, then drove an additional twenty-eight miles from the center of town to a dock marker bearing the same number: twenty-eight. There they chartered a guide who promised to take them by boat to Little Torch Key.

They discovered that the post office on the island was a contract station built beside one of the local watering holes. The clientele of the bar was a motley crew, who gave Able Team a critical once-over.

"They look more like burnt-out, over-the-hill beach bums who couldn't put up much of a fight if their lives depended on it," Blancanales whispered to Schwarz. None of the men were Asian.

They retrieved the final green envelope without any trouble. The clue was in English this time: Texas, Suckers.

As they walked out of one of the post office's side access corridors, they were confronted by two nervous Vietnamese teenagers. Able Team was caught off guard by the barefoot boys, who couldn't have been more than seventeen or eighteen years old. They looked as if they'd been camping out on the beach all week, but instead of fishing poles they now brandished sawed-off shotguns.

"Hand it over!" they demanded.

"Hand what over?" Blancanales asked coldly, unimpressed with their weapons.

"Whatever you took out of one of the postal boxes in there," one of the youths said, forcing his unruly black bangs out of his eyes and thrusting out his chin defiantly, hoping to reinforce his tough-guy image.

"Sure," Schwarz said, throwing a handful of junk mail onto the ground at their feet.

Momentarily distracted, the youths were quickly disarmed when Lyons sprang into action, throwing a flying body block that brought both boys down. He quickly subdued them, using one of the LAPD's outlawed choke holds.

21

Four Asians—two men and two women—made their way down one winding corridor after another until they reached a room marked: Chief of Detectives—Miami Police Department.

The two men were clad in expensive sport jackets; the two women in fashionable dresses. All four were well groomed. The men carried automatics in shoulder holsters; the women, snub-nosed .38s in their handbags. They appeared to be in their mid-thirties. Silently they stared through the glass partition in the door for a tense second or two before one of the women finally knocked.

A tall Hispanic sitting on the edge of a desk inside the office reached over and swung the door open. "Enter at your own risk, grunts."

The four Asians rushed in, expressions reflecting irritation at their sudden, unexpected summoning to the chief's office. They scanned the four intruders' faces, gauging intent, or trying to.

"Carl," the tall Hispanic said as he resumed his perch on the desktop, "allow me to introduce Detectives Nguyen and Tran." The two Asian men nodded. "And Detectives Lu and Pham." The women nodded. In sequence. Coldly. Robotic.

Ironman read the look in their narrowed eyes: *We're busy. We were on our way out to bust some felon. Who are these civilians you're wasting our time with?* Yeah, he knew the look. He'd been there before. He could sympathize, but didn't.

Lyons had just gotten off the hot line with Hal Brognola. The Chief had advised him that Tran Van Thieu, code name Numbnuts, was not only determined to remain silent, but had committed suicide by hanging himself. One tidbit of information he did surrender before his death, however, involved a Vietnamese Secret Police major by the name of Truong. Brognola sent a dossier on the Communist cop to Lyons via the Miami PD fax.

At that very moment Carl was staring down at a hard copy of the Vietnamese major's face. Also attached was a synopsis regarding the Phi-Chau Gang and Truong's connection to them.

At least now we know who we're dealing with, Lyons thought to himself as he ripped the fax paper to shreds.

"What's up, Chief?" the taller female asked as she inspected Haley Klein, who, in turn, checked out the Asian woman.

"This matter I'm about to bring before you is of the highest priority," the senior detective said. "National security is involved. Now I'm not going to delve into specifics, but remember that nothing discussed in this room today leaves this room. Ever. *Comprende?*"

"Understood," they all said, nodding routinely.

A portable chalkboard stood between the strangers and the investigators. The chief of detectives flipped it over. All eyes darted to the two groups of words:

Bay Sao Cai Den Tho
Hoa Son Khau Cai Vinh Anh Trang

"Does the first line mean anything to any of you?"

"Tell us what it would mean to a Vietnamese," Lyons added as he stared at the combination of words.

"Sure," Detective Pham said, nodding. "The Temple of Seven Stars."

"That's all?" Lyons demanded. "The Temple of Seven Stars?"

"Yes, sir. The line below it seems to be the Vietnamese equivalent of Crater Bay and Moonlight. Though I'm sure the writer meant Moonbeam, not Moonlight."

"There's no precise translation for *moonbeam* in Vietnamese," Detective Lu reminded her.

"Yes, of course. You're right, Wendy."

"Crater Bay and Moonlight, or Moonbeam," Lyons said, scratching at the stubble on his chin as he pondered the three words. "I wonder what they could mean, what reference they could have to this whole affair or—"

"I don't know what you guys are working on," Detective Pham interrupted, "but the Temple of Seven Stars is located at a place called Crater Bay near Moonbeam, Texas."

"You're familiar with it?" the chief of detectives asked, jumping up from the desktop. "Why didn't you say so?" he demanded.

Texas, Sucker... The last two secret words, from the post office box at Little Torch Key, seemed to float in front of Lyons's mind's eye, taunting him in glowing green neon— *emerald* green.

"The Temple of Seven Stars is no big thing," Detective Pham explained. "It's a modest but quite famous temple outside Galveston, Texas."

"Where the Viet fishermen had all the trouble with the locals a few years back?" Lyons asked. "The American shrimpers?"

"Yes. The Temple of Seven Stars is very important to religious Vietnamese. Many of them make a pilgrimage of sorts at least once in their lives, if only to touch the Buddha smuggled out of Vietnam several years before the fall of Saigon."

"Smuggled out of Vietnam?" Schwarz echoed.

"Yes. The Imperial City of Hue. Perhaps you've heard of it."

"I've heard of it," Blancanales said before storming from the room.

"Let's go," Lyons said, nodding to the others after jotting down the information in his pocket notebook. He scooped up the seven green envelopes on his way out. "And thanks!" he told the Miami chief of detectives.

"Anytime," the veteran street cop said, smiling as he remembered the priority-one phone call from Washington that had ordered him to "extend all courtesies" to the group just leaving.

Ten minutes later in the detective bureau down the hall Vice Investigator Gloria Pham entered one of the tiny interrogation cubicles and produced a telephone credit card. She searched her address book for several minutes—she hadn't called Uncle Dai-Ton in several years.

Detective Pham had been a naturalized American citizen for nearly nine years now, and a cop for most of that time. She knew that what she was doing might be construed as being wrong by her supervisor, and those four agents from Washington.

Detective Pham knew that something evil was about to befall the Temple of Seven Stars in Texas, and she knew that many of her uncle's followers visited the sacred shrine on a daily basis. She felt it was her duty to warn the man who had been so good to her over the years, financing her college tuition, seeing to it that she passed the Miami PD background investigation with flying colors, ensuring none of the underworld denizens harmed his favorite niece. Gloria Pham knew all this.

However, she didn't recognize the voice on the other end of the line at the Pho '90 Restaurant in Westminster, California.

"Uncle Dai-Ton not here," an old woman in a bad mood informed her. "He go Texas."

"Galveston?"

"Yes. You know place? Bay Sao Cai Den Tho."

"I know the place. Do you have a phone number where I can reach him?"

"No phone number. You go in person. Everyone go in person. That monk's law. You understand?"

"Yes, I think I do. I understand now. Thank you...thank you for all your help."

Detective Pham broke the connection. She knew her Uncle Dai-Ton was an important man and, although she wasn't assigned to the Asian gang detail, she suspected he might be involved in some questionable business dealings. She had no idea he commanded the brave freedom fighters known as Tu Do Luc Quan. She did know he was rumored to have been a senior commandant of the Resistance at one time or another. Gloria Pham also didn't know that Vietnamese Secret Police Major Truong had bugged several phones in Orange County's Little Saigon, including that of the Resistance's stateside contact point—the Pho '90 Restaurant.

Detective Pham wasn't sure what she should do. She couldn't just pack up and fly to Texas to warn an uncle she hadn't seen in five years. Warn him of what? That four agents were rushing to Galveston on some sort of secret mission that might release the forces of evil upon the Temple of Seven Stars?

She searched through her address book until her eyes locked onto the name and phone number of an ex-boyfriend. He was a man she remained on good speaking terms with. An American. A Vietnam veteran her Uncle Dai-Ton had disapproved of because she had moved in with him during college. Only her decision to relocate to Miami had separated them. She didn't care for all the violent drug czars and crazy ex-cons she found here, but the climate in Miami reminded her of Old Saigon.

Detective Pham dialed the New York City number. A voice on the other end of the line answered, "Adventurers Club."

"May I speak to Mr. Donovan, please?"

"Big Don Donovan?" the gruff voice boomed in her ear.

"Yes," she replied meekly. There was no hint in her frail voice that she had blown away two gunmen attempting to rape a liquor store clerk in Little Havana only the week before.

"He's outta town." There was absolutely no compassion in the man's tone. "I think he said Beirut. Or maybe it was Bangkok. Yeah, Beirut or Bangkok—take your pick, honey."

"Could you please tell him Gloria called? Gloria Pham."

"Gloria?"

"Yes."

"Hold on."

"What?"

"He's here. Big Don's never here for anyone unless Gloria calls."

"Unless Gloria calls?"

"That's what he told me. Hold on. I'll get him."

ABLE TEAM ARRIVED in Crater Bay about an hour after the massacre. The Temple of Seven Stars was located on an isolated hilltop overlooking Galveston Bay—so far from the surrounding communities that no one had witnessed the slaughter of innocent worshipers. Apparently no one had paid any attention to the din of sporadic gunfire even when it reached a dull crescendo a few minutes before midnight.

The bodies of several monks and more than a dozen visitors—all Vietnamese—lay around the temple grounds in grotesque positions, their limbs twisted unnaturally. Able

Team found a bloodbath when they arrived at approximately 1:00 a.m.

"No," Klein whispered, bringing a palm to her lips. She was aghast at the carnage.

"What do we do now?" Gadgets whispered to Ironman as they moved in the direction of the glowing pagoda. "We're obviously too late."

"Maybe. Maybe not. We fan out. Secure the perimeter. Take a body count. Search the temple."

A shiver went through Haley as she watched their CAR-15 barrels moving slowly through the gray mist—tinted an eerie shade by the glow from the Temple of Seven Stars.

"There's not enough of us to secure the perimeter," Blancanales muttered. "You know that."

"Just—"

Ironman's reply was cut short as a burst of bullets sprayed the ground near them. Several bullets struck one of the dead bodies, splattering them with crimson-soaked chunks of flesh and gristle.

"Did you see where it came from?" Lyons demanded after they took cover behind a pile of lifeless bodies.

Haley stared into the bulging, unblinking eyes of a dead Vietnamese woman. "No," she said, her voice cracking as her own eyes shifted to the gaping hole between the woman's breasts. The policewoman knew she was looking at an ugly exit wound that had torn the woman's blouse down the middle and ripped the inseam of her breasts from her sternum and rib cage, but it looked as if someone had carved the poor girl's heart out! "No, I didn't see...where it...came from...." she said haltingly.

Lyons reached forward and flicked wisps of hair from the nape of the dead woman's neck. A hissing cobra tattoo was revealed. "Looks like both sides took casualties here tonight." He lifted a tiny gold amulet from around the woman's throat. Its inscription read Coral.

Blancanales sent a five-round burst from his CAR-15 out toward the crest supporting the pagoda. He rolled hard to his right, changing magazines with the move, inserting a banana clip containing nothing but silver tracers. Moving up onto one knee beside a sand-filled oil drum, he brought the rifle to his shoulder and directed a constant stream of glowing, white-hot bullets out along the hillside's black outline. Shadows seemed to shift around out there, but he knew it was just his eyes playing games with him, and he tried to stare off to one side or the other while concentrating on his original target.

"Fantastic," Gadgets muttered under his breath at the light show. "That was beautiful!"

"Give it up!" Lyons shouted at the top of his lungs. "Whoever you are, throw down your weapon and let's talk. Man to man!"

"You foolish Americans can talk to this!" a voice with a heavy Asian accent shouted back, and several short bursts from an AK-47 assault rifle stitched the ground in front of Ironman.

Able Team responded with concentrated bursts from its trio of CAR-15s. Three laserlike bursts swept the hilltop around the Temple of Seven Stars.

After the shooting stopped, the Asian resumed yelling down at them. "Where is it?" he demanded. "I have searched everywhere! I have searched everyone! But I can't find it!"

"Where's what?" Lyons shouted as Schwarz and Blancanales crawled closer to the hillside.

"Don't toy with me. Let me have what I've come here for and I'll let you leave with your lives!"

"You've got to be kidding!" Lyons said, laughing.

"We're going to tear you into little strips!" Blancanales threatened. "By the time we're through with you, even your mother won't recognize what's left."

"The treasure belongs to the Vietnamese people!" Major Truong proclaimed as his silhouette appeared atop the hill, directly in front of the Temple of Seven Stars. "Not to these so-called refugees. They are nothing but traitors!"

"Tell it to the United Nations!" Blancanales said, bringing his rifle to his shoulder and taking aim.

"Wait!" Lyons called out. "Let him say his piece!"

"The President's Prize belongs to us!" Truong said, raising a clenched fist. "It belongs to the true patriots! Allow us to return it to the homeland! Allow the great Ho's soul to rest!"

"We don't know what the hell you're talking about!" Gadgets shouted, taking aim at Truong's chest. "But you can sure explain it to us!"

"Are you talking about the emeralds?" Haley, who was closer to Truong now than any of them, asked. "The ten million in emeralds stolen from your country?"

Truong erupted into almost boisterous laughter. "There are no emeralds, you fools!" he insisted. "Only the President's Prize! And it must be returned to the president!"

"What the hell's he rambling on about?" Schwarz demanded.

"The president?" Klein called back to them. "Could he be working for *our* president? I mean, could he be a double agent?"

"He's talking about the president of North Vietnam, baby, not the U.S.," Lyons said. "He's talking about President Ho!"

Suddenly Blancanales rose to his feet and, firing from the hip, charged the shadowy man on the hilltop. Truong fired back, but Politician was a better shot. Rounds danced around the secret police major's boots and he dropped back out of sight, only to reappear again behind a stack of bodies halfway down the hillside.

"All this carnage," Lyons said as he shifted alongside two of the corpses he himself had claimed for cover. "The bastard couldn't have gunned down all these people by himself." Ironman noted that there were five bodies clustered around him—five men in their fifties wearing business suits. The sport jacket had been completely ripped from one man's back. Along his right shoulder a tattoo of three words was visible: Mot Bo Bay.

The Cult of Seven.

The rest of One-eyed Ngoc's buddies had finally met their maker. "And none of us is any closer to the documents—or the emeralds. *If* either exists..."

At his feet was a sixth corpse, its head missing. Tiny Roman numerals were embroidered across his collar in blue, proclaiming the number *714*. General Pham? There was no way of telling. Not yet.

He glanced back over at Truong. The Vietnamese whose influence had dogged them from Angel Fire, New Mexico, to Freeport, Maine, to an island off the coast of Florida, was flexing his power again. Somewhere between forty and fifty men had appeared behind the major. They, too, brandished AK-47 assault rifles.

Able Team was outnumbered and outgunned.

22

Blancanales had crawled to the ground-floor foyer of the Temple of Seven Stars, not knowing exactly where the elusive gunman had disappeared to, but well aware he might find some of the answers to the mystery within the pagoda itself.

Rising into a combat crouch, he quickly cleared the first level and began climbing the spiral stairwell to the second floor. Within seconds he was searching the top floor, staring at a surreal image of Buddha drifting back and forth, ever so slightly, behind silver clouds of floating incense.

The temple's altar and ancestral shrine were heavy with mysticism and holiness, but there was certainly no treasure to be found there. Blancanales searched inside every conceivable hiding place. Finally it became evident they would find no emeralds or documents at Crater Bay.

When he leaned out through a bamboo curtain to advise the others, Blancanales spotted Truong's private army of Phi-Chau Gang fighters. In the distance there was nothing. Silence. A deafening quiet. There would be no help. Not tonight. Lyons and the others might be able to hold off Truong long enough for some insomniac out there to finally call the police to complain about all the shooting. Eventually they'd get help. Reinforcements would arrive.

But that was only in the movies. In real life the cavalry was often too late.

The only thing Blancanales could do now was to keep searching. He silently returned to the ground floor and began prowling the shadows, searching . . . searching for anything.

In the distance he heard the distinct sound of children crying, and he crawled in that direction. The sound of weeping children quickly grew louder, flashing him back, without warning, to a search-and-destroy mission he'd participated in back in Vietnam. It had been twenty years ago, but in his mind he could still clearly see the crib and the tunnel entrance hidden beneath it and the dark maze of catacombs beckoning him.

When Blancanales burst into the building behind the Temple of Seven Stars, his eyes focused on the crib. He ignored the hysterical children—most would be orphans now. He sealed his ears to their cries, as Truong must have done, and lifted the children out of the crib. Then he moved the crib aside. Déjà-vu, dude.

Below a straw mat a trapdoor beckoned. It wasn't secured, and soon he was dropping down into the black pit, feeling himself bounce around on a trampolinelike series of nets and ropes until he regained his balance by grasping a wooden ladder protruding from the earthen wall.

The underground chamber was small—no larger than fifteen by twenty feet, and less than thirty feet deep. Water seeped through fissures in the earthen wall. They were obviously near the ocean here. At high tide the tunnels probably flooded.

In the center of the chamber a tiny gas lantern glowed inside a common "good luck" altar. Adorned with dozens of green candlesticks, it had been erected to scare away any cave demons who might take notice of and want to steal the children being harbored above.

Blancanales sensed this was it, and more memories of Vietnam flooded back to haunt him as he took hold of the chest-high altar and removed the candlestick shrine.

Inside the altar's teakwood frame he found a lacquer-wood box. It was about the size of a typewriter. Blancanales removed a commando dagger from the sheath on his leg and began prying at the box's ancient lock. A shiver tore through him as the clasp broke free and the shriveled hands came into view. Two hands severed at the wrists.

The hands of Ho Chi Minh.

THE SHOOTING RESUMED shortly thereafter.

Blancanales was careful to conceal the President's Prize before leaving the tunnel chamber to rejoin Able Team. Outside, his people were quickly being surrounded and outmaneuvered.

"I'm telling you!" he could hear Lyons shouting. "We don't know anything about it!"

"You're lying!" Truong screamed maniacally. "But it is too late now! Too late for all of us!"

"At least let the girl go!"

"You're all going to die here tonight!" the secret police major insisted before leading the final charge.

"It was nice knowing you!" Lyons and Gadgets both said, huddling back, with Klein between them.

"I'm down to three banana clips!" Schwarz announced. "How about you guys?"

"Half that!" Ironman shouted above the din of automatic weapons fire.

"I lost my weapon in all the commotion!" Klein cried out.

"Here!" Blancanales said, crashing into the muck beside them. He slammed a pistol into Haley's hands. "Don't fire until you see their bloodshot eyes!"

"Is that what John Wayne would say?" Klein challenged with a forced smile.

"No! Sean Connery!"

Concussion grenades began exploding all around them, quickly disorienting the men of Able Team and their lone female companion. But it suddenly appeared that all hope wasn't lost—the hand-thrown bombs were scattering Truong's men, as well.

Four Land Rovers loaded down with mercenaries roared up to the temple. They were led by Big Don Donovan, Peter K. Nunn and a tall blond woman named Joan Andrews.

Professional soldiers of fortune quickly dismounted from the all-terrain vehicles, engaging Truong's gangsters in more than a few running gun battles and, eventually, hand-to-hand combat. Able Team joined the fray, and the disorganized, unmotivated Vietnamese were quickly rounded up.

It was Carl Lyons who located Truong. The Vietnamese Secret Police major was crouching behind a pile of bodies atop the crater's rim, sighting his American-made M-700 sniper rifle on Haley Klein's chest when Ironman pounced.

The commando's knees slamming against Truong's back were enough to knock the air from his lungs and the fight out of his determination. Gagging, he rolled over onto his back and surrendered.

As the final rifle shots were being fired, Blancanales could be seen standing in front of the Temple of Seven Stars, screaming out his war cry, purging his soul of pain and sorrow over the loss of South Vietnam so many years ago, raising a clenched fist, now, to victory.

EPILOGUE

Haley Klein flushed cherry-red. She found it hard to believe she was in the same room as the President of the United States! Lyons, Blancanales, Schwarz and a man she'd just met—Hal Brognola—were also present.

"There never were any emeralds, Mr. President," Brognola said. "And the documents recovered with the severed hands substantiate your claim that a U.S.-sanctioned death squad did accidentally kill an important Vietnamese ally in the 1950s."

"The official line was always that the man was killed in a plane crash, his body never recovered," the President said as he moved to a large window and stared out into the distance.

"But the actual story came out at that temple tragedy in Moonbeam, Texas," Brognola continued. "The man was a spy...a double agent who *had* to be killed. You, Mr. President, weren't involved with the actual termination."

"Did you ever find General Pham?" the President asked.

"We think so," Brognola said. "There were some forty bodies recovered and—"

"Civilians?"

"Yes, sir. A number of the bodies haven't been identified yet. A few of the surviving monks tentatively identified Pham, although they couldn't be positive. The head is still missing. I've got Kruger at the Pentagon coordinating a fingerprint scan with the FBI, but it'll probably prove inconclusive." Brognola chuckled. "You know how those things go, sir. Hell, the General may be back in Thailand right now, for all we know, leading the Resistance in another hit-and-run raid on the Vietnamese Secret Police. He's crafty. Cashed in that ten million in gems clear back in 1975 to assist in funding the freedom fighters after his family's assets were seized by the new Communist regime. Yeah, I'll bet he's leading a brave group of freedom fighters on a midnight raid through the streets of Saigon at this very minute!"

"Let's hope so. Yes, let's hope so," the President said, returning to the lacquer-wood box sitting on his desk. "And you have this Truong character in custody?"

"He's being debriefed at length, sir."

"Good."

The President slowly opened the box's lid and peered down at the severed hands of Ho Chi Minh. "Vietnam's been a wound in this nation's heart and soul long enough," he said.

"Yes, sir. We quite agree," Brognola said.

"Those damn Communists!" the President said, his fingers drumming on the lacquer-wood lid impatiently. "Always twisting the knife in our back, always producing one more set of remains, one more MIA or POW body to be used as a bargaining chip."

"They're still hoping we'll rebuild their country," Brognola said. "Their leaders just have a rather twisted way of trying to get our cooperation."

"The Vietnamese say that this is a prize more valuable than even emeralds or diamonds—the severed hands of Ho Chi Minh!" the President told the group. "For in Vietnamese legend, and correct me if I'm wrong, anyone possessing the severed hands of a dead person is said to hold that individual's destiny in their power. And if the individual is a much-revered leader, the fate of the entire country and its current leadership can be controlled."

"That's how the story goes, sir," Blancanales said, nodding somberly.

"They always want to bargain, using the remains of our missing sons and brothers," the President said, shaking his head with disgust. "Well, now *we* have something to bargain with—the hands of Ho Chi Minh."

"We Vietnam veterans have waited a long time for something like this," Blancanales declared.

The President extended his hand. "Welcome home, son."

Introducing Max Horn. He's not your typical cop. But then,
nothing's typical in the year 2025.

HORN

HOT ZONE

BEN SLOANE

The brutal attack left New York Police Detective Max Horn
clinging to life and vowing to seek vengeance on the
manic specter who murdered his wife and young son.
Now, thanks to cold hard cash and the genius of an
underground techno-doc, Max is a new man with a few
new advantages—titanium skin and biomechanical
limbs hard-wired to his central nervous system.

On an asteroid called New Pittsburgh, Max walks a new
beat...and in a horrible twist of fate comes face-to-face
with the man who killed his family.

Look for HORN #1—HOT ZONE in March wherever
paperbacks are sold because once you meet Max Horn,
you'll never forget him.

GOLD
EAGLE

HORN-1

TAKE 'EM NOW

FOLDING SUNGLASSES
FROM GOLD EAGLE

Mean up your act with these tough, street-smart shades. Practical, too, because they fold 3 times into a handy, zip-up polyurethane pouch that fits neatly into your pocket. Rugged metal frame. Scratch-resistant acrylic lenses. Best of all, they can be yours for only $6.99.

MAIL YOUR ORDER TODAY.

Send your name, address, and zip code, along with a check or money order for just $6.99 + .75¢ for postage and handling (for a total of $7.74) payable to Gold Eagle Reader Service. (New York and Iowa residents please add applicable sales tax.)

Remove from pouch.

untold once

untold twice

and they're ready to wear

GOLD EAGLE Gold Eagle Reader Service
901 Fuhrmann Blvd.
P.O. Box 1396
Buffalo, N.Y. 14240-1396

GES-1A

Offer not available in Canada.

Illegal nuclear testing in Antarctica sends Phoenix Force Down Under when a maniacal plot threatens global destruction.

SUPER PHOENIX FORCE #3

COLD DEAD

GAR WILSON

The two superpowers suspect one another of illegal nuclear testing in Antarctica when the bodies of two murdered scientists show high levels of radiation in their systems.

It's a crisis situation that leads Phoenix Force to New Zealand, where a madman's growing arsenal of nuclear weapons is destined for sale on the international black market....

Don't miss the riveting confrontation in COLD DEAD when it explodes onto the shelves at your favorite retail outlet in April, or reserve your copy for March shipping by sending your name, address, zip or postal code along with a check or money order for $4.70 (includes 75¢ postage and handling) payable to Gold Eagle Books:

In the U.S.
901 Fuhrmann Blvd.
Box 1325
Buffalo, NY 14269-1325

In Canada
P.O. Box 609
Fort Erie, Ontario
L2A 5X3

GOLD EAGLE ®

Please specify book title with your order.

SPF3-1